Cuba
and
His Teddy Bear

by Reinaldo Povod

A SAMUEL FRENCH ACTING EDITION

MUSIC USE NOTE

Licensees are solely responsible for obtaining formal written permission from copyright owners to use copyrighted music in the performance of this play and are strongly cautioned to do so. If no such permission is obtained by the licensee, then the licensee must use only original music that the licensee owns and controls. Licensees are solely responsible and liable for all music clearances and shall indemnify the copyright owners of the play and their licensing agent, Samuel French, Inc., against any costs, expenses, losses and liabilities arising from the use of music by licensees.

IMPORTANT BILLING AND CREDIT
REQUIREMENTS

All producers of *CUBA AND HIS TEDDY BEAR must* give credit to the Author of the Play in all programs distributed in connection with performances of the Play, and in all instances in which the title of the Play appears for the purposes of advertising, publicizing or otherwise exploiting the Play and/or a production. The name of the Author *must* appear on a separate line on which no other name appears, immediately following the title and *must* appear in size of type not less than fifty percent of the size of the title type.

LONGACRE THEATRE

A Shubert Organization Theatre

Gerald Schoenfeld, *Chairman*   Bernard B. Jacobs, *President*

JOSEPH PAPP presents

ROBERT DE NIRO   RALPH MACCHIO   BURT YOUNG

in

CUBA & HIS TEDDY BEAR

by **REINALDO POVOD**

directed by **BILL HART**

with

PAUL CALDERON   **WANDA DE JESUS**   **NESTOR SERRANO**

and

MICHAEL CARMINE

Scenery by	Costumes by	Lighting by
DONALD EASTMAN	GABRIEL BERRY	ANNE E. MILITELLO

Associate Producer **JASON STEVEN COHEN**

A NEW YORK SHAKESPEARE FESTIVAL PRODUCTION

The Producers wish to express their appreciation to Theatre Development Fund for its support of this production.

CAST

(in order of speaking)

Cuba	ROBERT DE NIRO
Teddy	RALPH MACCHIO
Jackie	BURT YOUNG
Redlights	NESTOR SERRANO
Lourdes	WANDA DE JESUS
Che	MICHAEL CARMINE
Dealer	PAUL CALDERON

"A man must descend very low to find the force to rise again."—Hasidic poem

UNDERSTUDIES

Understudies never substitute for listed players unless a specific announcement
for the appearance is made at the time of the performance.

For Redlights, Dealer—Antonio Aponte; for Che—Paul Calderon; for Teddy—Eddie Castrodad; for Cuba, Jackie—Tom Mardirosian; for Lourdes—Olivia Negron.

THERE WILL BE ONE FIFTEEN-MINUTE INTERMISSION

CHARACTERS

CUBA
TEDDY
JACKIE
REDLIGHTS
LOURDES
CHE
DEALER

TIME

September. The present.

PLACE

A tenement apartment
on the Lower East Side of Manhattan.

To my grandmother, Lilia Esther Povod

"A man must descend very low
to find the force to rise again."
                    —Hasidic poem

CUBA AND HIS TEDDY BEAR

ACT I

CUBA'S apartment. An early afternoon in September. The apartment is a comfortable, well-ordered place. The main playing area is the living room, furnished with a plastic-covered sofa, a coffee table and a medium-sized wall mirror in a large frame. Up against the wall in one corner is an altar — a small table — on which stands a two-foot-high statue of the Virgin Mary, "La Caridad del Cobre" [Our Lady of the Cove]. The altar displays an unusual and startling use of color: it is covered with a vivid tablecloth, and brightly colored objects surround the statue — little play toys, painted seashells, rocks — along with offerings of a small shot glass containing Bacardi dark rum, a half-smoked cigar and a brandy snifter with water in it.

Upstage left, a passageway leads offstage to the bathroom and CUBA'S bedroom. Downstage left, we see a section of TEDDY'S bedroom. A small bed and an old-fashioned bureau are clearly visible. There is no door between TEDDY'S room and the living room but a door leads offstage to CUBA'S room and the bathroom. The area is lit by a lamp on the bureau.

Off the living room, stage right, is the kitchen, with a small table, a sink and refrigerator, and a door leading to the outside hallway. The kitchen window (the only window in the set) has no shade and is hung with faded yellow curtains; it is open and through it we can see the worn brick wall of the

*building next door. The kitchen is lit by an overhead bulb but
the main source of light in this area is the sunshine stream-
ing through the window.*

*Two carpets of different design and color cover the kitchen
and living-room floors. The living-room carpet is dark and
worn, clearly showing its age. The kitchen carpet is bright
and new.*

*At the start of the scene, TEDDY and JACKIE are sitting in
the living room. CUBA is standing, wearing only shower
slippers and a towel wrapped tightly around his waist. A
long silence as CUBA and JACKIE stare at TEDDY.*

CUBA. *(accusingly)* Ya thinkin'.
TEDDY. I'm not thinkin', Pop.
CUBA. I saw you.
TEDDY. I wasn't.
JACKIE. You were.
CUBA. *(to JACKIE)* You saw 'im.
JACKIE. Your eyes went like this. *(He makes a face.)*
CUBA. You were thinkin'.
TEDDY. I wasn't, Pop.
JACKIE. Your eyes went like this. *(He makes a face.)*
CUBA. Whattaya thinkin' about?
TEDDY. Nothing, Pop, nothing.
CUBA. *(slowly for effect)* What are you thinkin' about?
TEDDY. Nothing.
CUBA. Swear. Swear you're not thinkin' about no-
thin'.
TEDDY. ... I swear.

CUBA. What's that face for?

TEDDY. I ain't got a face.

CUBA. *(to JACKIE)* You see it?

JACKIE. He went like this. *(He makes a face.)*

CUBA. You were thinkin'.

TEDDY. I wasn't thinking.

CUBA. Whatta hardhead.

JACKIE. What do you think you wanna be — anything?

CUBA. What do you think about being a cop?

JACKIE. You gotta be twenty-one to be a cop.

CUBA. He can go to college.

JACKIE. He can do that.

CUBA. He'll do it, he's a smart kid. *(to TEDDY)* Sit up straight. Look at 'im—now he's mad at me. I'm trying to teach him sump'm—I'm trying to teach you sump'm. What do you think about a lawyer? Lawyers make a lot of money. *(No response from TEDDY.)* Nothin'. He's the only guy I know who's always thinkin' about nothing.

TEDDY. I know what I wanna do Pop.

CUBA. Oh yeah? Tell me—I wanna know if you know what you're talking about.

TEDDY. ...I will—I will Pop.

CUBA. I'm waiting—I got all the time in the world.

TEDDY. ...But not yet Pop, not just yet.

CUBA. I ain't got that much friggin' time.

TEDDY. I know—

CUBA. You know, you know. What do you know? *(A very awkward silence.)* Are you afraid of me....Ha?!

TEDDY. ...No.

CUBA. Are you afraid of Jackie? Instead of talking to

me—you wanna talk to Jackie? He's yer godfather. *(TEDDY shakes his head no.)* You gotta mouth don't you?

TEDDY. Yes.

CUBA. Let's hear it.

TEDDY. No.

CUBA. You don't wanna talk to me. You don't wanna talk to Jackie. Do you believe this guy? He don't feel like talking about it. Listen pal, lemme tell ya, you're not s'posed to be afraid of me—

TEDDY. It's not that, Pop, I already told ya—

CUBA. I will never hurt you. *(slowly for effect)* I will never hurt you. I talk to you this way 'cos I'm talkin' to you like a man. You know what I'm sayin'? I grew up on the street and you grew up here on the same block. It's my way of expressing, awright? You ain't a kid—yer fifteen.

TEDDY. I'm sixteen—I'll be seventeen in a few weeks—

CUBA. Sixteen, look at that shit. You wanna go into the army?

TEDDY. No.

CUBA. The army will make a man outta you— *(to JAC-KIE)* or is it the marines—well it don't matter—the service will straighten yer shit out.

TEDDY. No I don't wanna go in the service Pop.

JACKIE. They take care of everything when yer in there—you don't have to worry about a thin'.

CUBA. I didn't have a police record, I woulda been in the army. I swear, if I didn't have a long friggin' record I woulda had it made by now. How 'bout the navy? Yer brother is in the navy.

TEDDY. No thanks Pop.

CUBA. The navy will be good fer you.

JACKIE. Yeah. Look at Popeye.

CUBA. If we want anything outta you—we'll rattle yer cage.

JACKIE. Hey Cuba, go screw yerself.

CUBA. I don't want you becoming a bum—you understand?

TEDDY. Yeah—yes.

CUBA. You heard what I said?...You're not off in limbo? It sunk in...? *(to JACKIE)* Sometimes I don't know what goes on in his mind.

JACKIE. At his age—they're all like that. There's nothin' wrong with him, he's a good kid.

CUBA. Hey. I *know* that. *(to TEDDY)* You remember what I said? What did I say?

TEDDY. You don't want me becoming a bum.

CUBA. I'm yer friend. Don't think of me as yer father. But yer best friend in the world. *(slowly for effect)* I am your friend.

TEDDY. Yes Pop.

CUBA. Nobody can be a better friend than me.

TEDDY. I know Pop.

CUBA. You got money—you got friends all over the place. You're broke, nobody wants you. Those same so-called friends don't wanna know you. Me, I'm always there.

TEDDY. Yeah, yes.

CUBA. Do you gotta friend who will pick yer nose—

TEDDY. What?

CUBA. Ha? You ain't got a friend like that?

TEDDY. No Pop.

CUBA. Sure you do.

JACKIE. Don't look at me.

TEDDY. I don't think so, Pop.

CUBA. Whatta you think I been talkin' to you about?

TEDDY. Uh-huh.

CUBA. Me! I'll pick yer nose.

TEDDY. Would you pick Jackie's nose?

JACKIE. C'mon, Cuba, pick me a winner.

CUBA. Jackie's Jewish. He picks it even when he doesn't have to.

JACKIE. Take a shit an' fall on it, awright Cuba.

CUBA. You got what I was saying?

TEDDY. Yes, Pop.

CUBA. What did I say?

TEDDY. You said that a friend is someone who sees a piece of snot hanging outta your nose and he picks it for you.

JACKIE. That's a hell of a friend—

CUBA. It grabs you?

JACKIE. Yeah, it's really deep, Cuba, it grabs me.

CUBA. Good.

JACKIE. Right between the legs. Listen, Cuba, I gotta talk to you. Commere, kid... *(He inserts his hand into his pocket and withdraws a roll of bills.)* Take a few bucks, here... *(TEDDY peels off a few dollar bills. He hands back the money.)* Let your old man and me talk some business.

CUBA. *(to TEDDY)* Whachu got there, lemme see? *(Checks how much money TEDDY took.)* That's all you took? —When ya suppose to graduate?

TEDDY. This June.

CUBA. This June? Awright, lemme know. *(TEDDY*

shoves the money into his pocket and goes to his room. He takes his writing pad and pen off the bureau. JACKIE walks over to the record rack, takes out an album and sits at the coffee table. TEDDY starts to write on his pad. During the following dialogue, JACKIE takes a plastic bag containing cocaine from his pocket. He empties the contents out onto the album cover and with an old-fashioned straight razor proceeds to chop and divide the cocaine.) This guy I got—

JACKIE. The same guy you been talking to me about—

CUBA. That guy, yeah.

JACKIE. Who wants an ounce—

CUBA. Yeah, he wants an ounce twice a week—

JACKIE. Uh-huh.

CUBA. What?

JACKIE. Nothing. I can get you the ounces.

TEDDY. *(stops writing and reads aloud)* Words Said at a Time. By: Teddy Cuba. Out of control, my curses—like Mount Olympus—thundered up and jolted the Lord Almighty off his throne. No, I don't have a love for self-destruction, its just that losing brings out the sadist in me. —Or is it masochist? What the fuck is it? *(continues writing)*

CUBA. Don't gimme any headaches.

JACKIE. Cuba, hey, c'mon. Take it with mucho *(with a Spanish accent says:)* "take it easy." It's jus' you an' me, pal.

CUBA. I'm gonna be dealin' this coke—

JACKIE. I don't want to hear it.

CUBA. Wait a second—

JACKIE. That's your business. The less I know—

CUBA. Lemme finish.

JACKIE. The better it is for me. Keep me stupid.

CUBA. I'm just gonna be dealin'—

JACKIE. Keep me stupid.

CUBA. I'm gonna be dealin' directly to the guy. It's gonna be hit and run. Bang, here's yer ounce, let's go, gimme my money.

JACKIE. Sounds good, but you know that awready. I dunno why yer tellin' it to me.

CUBA. I wanna tell it to you.

JACKIE. You gotta steady customer coming twice a week—beautiful—it's good money.

CUBA. It is good money.

JACKIE. Yeah.

CUBA. Yeah.

JACKIE. Let's not talk about it. Let's see what happens.

CUBA. What's gonna happen? We're gonna make money.

JACKIE. Yeah.

CUBA. Yeah.

TEDDY. *(stops writing, reads aloud)* I slammed the basketball against the backboard, the guys laughing, "Hey, it's jus'a game." No, I told them. "Sore loser." I ain't a sore loser, I said to them in the same tone. "C'mon, man, get over yourself." No, this is God's fault. GODDAMNIT, I said outta control. GODDAMNIT. Damn You God. —That's too many Gods. —No, this is God's fault. Goddamn. Damn You God. You see, I don't mind losing but I hate losing to a scrub. I took my time walking back home from the gym. I took my time walking back home from the gym. *(continues writing)*

CUBA. All I want, Jackie—

JACKIE. *(Spells it out.)* M.O.N.E.Y.

CUBA. No, I'm sayin', I want you to keep this shit—the coke coming at me, fast and over the plate. No fucken curves.

JACKIE. I don't like that.

CUBA. I don't like it either.

JACKIE. I don't like what you said.

CUBA. Good. You know what, then don't do it.

JACKIE. Who you talking to? I ain't no two-dollar broad in a four-dollar world.

CUBA. I don't wanna be fucked.

JACKIE. Who's gonna fuck you?

CUBA. Don't fuck me.

TEDDY. *(reading aloud)* I decided to take the long way home. Down the picturesque Third Avenue: where barefoot 'ho's try to lure you with swollen ankles and smiling frowns. Third Avenue where no one waves. Second Avenue, Third Avenue, any ghetto avenue sparkles on account of the smashed pieces of glass and broken beer bottles—that, like the Lord of Hosts, resembles the brilliant stars. —Wow. *(continues writing)*

JACKIE. Cuba?

CUBA. I'm lissening.

JACKIE. I'm doing you a favor.

CUBA. You ain't doing me a favor.

JACKIE. I'm doing you a favor.

CUBA. You ain't gettin' nothin'? Yer hump.

JACKIE. I'm doing you a favor.

CUBA. You ain't gettin' nothin' outta my coke deal?

JACKIE. Yeah.

CUBA. Huh?

JACKIE. Yeah, I said.

CUBA. *(referring to the coke)* I don't need this.

JACKIE. I don't need this shit either.

CUBA. No, I don't need this at all. At all!

JACKIE. I lived before it—I can live after it.

CUBA. Next pinch I get, that's it for me. Adio' Cuba, three-time loser. Three-time loser—I might as well put my head b'tween my knees and kiss my ass good-bye.

TEDDY. *(reading aloud)* Outta jail, or a treatment center, in tight shorts, she approaches me. "Quiere?" You want some? No thank you. I don't like chicharrones, fried pigskins. The 'ho sinks a hungry bite into her chicharrones. Hmmm good, and gives me her beneath-the-moon smile—goes through me and ends with me grabbing my peepee in a strange fashion...grabbing my penis...grabbing my dick...grabbing my peepee in a strange fashion—or is it outta fear of castration? You never know with Third Avenue whores. I fold my arms in an attempt to ask her what she wants— but she beats me to the punch. "You wanna buy some methadone juice?"

JACKIE. You wanna meet the guy give me the coke?

TEDDY. No, thank you, I don't wanna buy methadone.

CUBA. No, I don't wanna know 'im.

TEDDY. "No, you don't?" she says to me. "That's too bad." And she walks away. *(continues writing)*

JACKIE. You don't wanna meet the guy who supplies me?

CUBA. I'm doing business only with you. Okay?

JACKIE. We do business.

CUBA. You and me. This way—God forbid anybody fucks up—I know who I'm doing time for.

JACKIE. Why yer busting my balls?

CUBA. I know you, you're a hard-on, Jackie. I don't wanna change in the quality of the coke. I don't wanna be caught short a gram—you're famous for that shit—don't tell me no.

JACKIE. Hey, Mister Magoo, I wanna be in business. Whachu got with this guy coming twice a week for two ounces of coke is a "black woman's dream." Money in the bank.

CUBA. No unnecessary shit.

JACKIE. None.

CUBA. I wanna make money.

JACKIE. We're gonna make money. Taste this. *(CUBA and JACKIE snort as TEDDY speaks.)*

TEDDY. *(reading aloud)* I felt sorry for the girl who wanted to sell me her methadone. I even felt a little guilty—I had a few dollars. But I don't need methadone—I don't have a drug habit. I watched her shake her "money-maker." Her ass. And I saw her thank her Lord Jesus for the bounty which he shares in this brightness of broken bottles and shattered glass. She patted her "money-maker." Smiled. At least she had that to fall back on. *(Said with contempt:)* 'Thank-God.'

CUBA. Teddy?

TEDDY. Pop?

CUBA. Commere.

TEDDY. *(entering the living room)* Commere?

CUBA. Get me an underwear.

TEDDY. An underwear?

CUBA. A nice pair.

TEDDY. A T-shirt, too?

CUBA. Get me a T-shirt. A nice one, somethin' that's not too wrinkled, somethin' that looks nice.

TEDDY. Awright.

CUBA. Please, okay?

TEDDY. Yeah, yes! *(He rushes into his room and pulls out one of the bureau drawers. Begins to search frantically for a pair of knee-length boxer shorts and an unwrinkled T-shirt.)*

CUBA. Where's yer ball-and-chain?

JACKIE. The same old shit.

CUBA. You kicked her out, or what?

JACKIE. I wanted her to say please. Please excuse me, you know? Please be quiet. Instead of shut the fuck up. Don't get me wrong, she's a beautiful woman, but things like that piss me off. Not even a good-morning. I'm up as a pup, I wanna jump on yer lap, say good morning to ya. All I hear from her is a fucken growl, I mean, she's a beautiful woman, who takes pleasure in knowing she pisses me off.

CUBA. She got her walkin' papers—

JACKIE. I gave her her walking papers, yeah.

(TEDDY enters with a T-shirt and pair of boxer shorts. He hands them to CUBA.)

JACKIE. She'll come back.

CUBA. *(To TEDDY, after scrutinizing the underwear.)* Whatta you call this? *(showing him the shorts)*

TEDDY. That's a hole, Pop.

JACKIE. I dunno.

CUBA. *(to TEDDY)* Yeah, that's a hole—that's a big hole. Is that the best you can do? Don't just look at me, is that the best you can do?

TEDDY. No.

CUBA. No what?

TEDDY. I can do better.

CUBA. Show me. *(He throws the shorts to TEDDY. To JACKIE.)* So she left you?

JACKIE. I said you wanna leave?...Leave. And then she left. *(TEDDY walks back into his room, over to the bureau, pulls out one of the drawers. Starts to search for a decent pair of shorts.)*

TEDDY. Pop?...Pop?

JACKIE. Yer kid.

CUBA. Yeah?

TEDDY. Who's gonna know you have a hole in your underwears?

CUBA. Me! I'm gonna know. *(CUBA puts on his T-shirt. JACKIE takes a quick snort.)*

JACKIE. I'm glad you brought that piece of snatch up.

CUBA. Who, yer wife?

JACKIE. You know what she said to me?

CUBA. Tell me.

JACKIE. I'm gonna tell ya. I bring her over a hamburger, french fries, and a vanilla milk shake.

CUBA. Yer a wonderful person.

JACKIE. She likes that crap. Me? I rather buy a pretzel and jump off the Brooklyn Bridge.

TEDDY. *(returning)* How's this, Pop?

CUBA. *(Takes the shorts, gives them a thorough going-over.)* It's awright, but it could be better.

TEDDY. It could always be better.

CUBA. Go 'head, Jackie, with what you were saying. *(to TEDDY)* What else? *(He puts the shorts on, throws the towel to TEDDY.)* Go 'head, I'm lissening, Jackie. *(He takes a snort of the coke.)*

TEDDY. Socks and shoes.

JACKIE. Lissen to this, Cuba.

CUBA. I'm lissening.

TEDDY. You want me to bring you a suit too?

JACKIE. She says to me—

CUBA. No, jus' gimme my shoes, and my socks.

JACKIE. —where's the straw? *(TEDDY starts to walk away.)*

CUBA. Bring me some cologne.

TEDDY. Cologne?

JACKIE. Cologne.

CUBA. Cologne. *(TEDDY exits to the bathroom and CUBA'S room.)*

JACKIE. Where's the straw, Cuba? This woman is outta her friggin' mind. I didn't bring a straw. I got no brains. I forgot the friggin' straws, so what? Get one from the kitchen yer wombat from a Florida swamp!

TEDDY. *(Returns with CUBA'S socks and shoes and his bottle of cologne.)* Here, Pop.

CUBA. Those socks cleans?

TEDDY. They smell clean. *(CUBA smells his socks.)*

JACKIE. She's on the bed—Christ, she looked like a fat hen on eggs—watching TV. *(CUBA puts on his socks and *shoes. TEDDY starts combing CUBA'S hair.)* The walk to the kitchen would do her a lot a good.

CUBA. Yeah.

JACKIE. Huh?

CUBA. Yeah, it's good for the heart. Walking is good for the heart.

JACKIE. She goes into the kitchen, she comes back with a face, I dunno if I should throw a bone at it, or kill the fucken thing?! Rosemary, I say, you tellin' me you brought back only one straw? Whatta 'bout me, I don't get a straw?

TEDDY. *(stops combing his father's hair)* You want the cologne, Pop?

JACKIE. I bought me an orange soda.

CUBA. *(to TEDDY)* Yeah. *(to JACKIE)* And you can't drink yer soda—

JACKIE. No, I can't drink my soda without a straw, that's right. *(TEDDY unscrews the top from the bottle of cologne, pours out a handful.)*

CUBA. *(To TEDDY, bending down for him.)* Be nice. *(TEDDY proceeds to pat CUBA's face lightly.)*

JACKIE. The soda was in one of them containers, you know, with the plastic top, gotta little hole in it, for the straw.

CUBA. All you gotta do is take the top offa it.

JACKIE. I don't wannt do that. When I take a sip, I get a mouthful of ice. That's no fun. I want a straw. She knew I needed a straw. Where's my straw? I asked her. I wanna straw. *(using a high-pitched, nasal female voice)* Get it yourself.

CUBA. Yeah, that's right.

JACKIE. No.

CUBA. She wasn't gonna get you one.

JACKIE. That's why I told her to fucken leave. At once!

TEDDY. Pop, you want yer suit?

CUBA. Yeah.

JACKIE. *(to TEDDY)* Yeah.

TEDDY. What color suit, Pop?

CUBA. I dunno, take out my—

TEDDY. Pierre Cardin?

CUBA. No, get me my...dark pinstripe...

TEDDY. Pierre Cardin.

CUBA. Yeah...Pierre. *(TEDDY takes the cologne and exits to the bathroom and CUBA'S room.)*

JACKIE. You gettin' all dressed up?

CUBA. To see this guy who wants the coke. I don't want him to think he's dealin' with a bum. You finish snorting my shit? I can't give this guy two measly blows!

JACKIE. No, of course you can't, I know.

CUBA. So stop snorting my shit, awright? I gotta give this guy a nice sample.

JACKIE. I know.

CUBA. He's gonna think I'm a guy who stands in hallways dealing, if I got nothing to give him—

JACKIE. No, no yer right.

CUBA. Yeah.

JACKIE. Yeah-yeah, I'm sorry.

CUBA. He's gonna think—

JACKIE. Yeah-yeah.

CUBA. He's dealing with a guy—

JACKIE. Yeah.

Cuba. —who's got his head up his ass and he's taking his temperature.

Jackie. Yeah!

Cuba. You know?

Jackie. I know. But lemme finish, Cuba, with what I was tellin' you about my old lady.

(TEDDY returns with his father's gray suit. JACKIE sneaks in a blow of cocaine as CUBA turns to take his suit from TEDDY.)

Teddy. This is it, right, Pop?

Jackie. So I tell her, Cuba, sports fan, lissen to this...

Cuba. *(smoothes his suit with his hand)* I'm lissening. *(referring to JACKIE'S snorting)* You finish? *(He stomps loudly on the floor to kill a cockroach which fell out of the suit.)*

Jackie. With what I was saying?

Cuba. Jesus—

Jackie. Yeah.

Cuba. *Snorting.*

Jackie. Sure.

Cuba. Yeah. You think I'm gonna pay you for what you snorted?

Jackie. You took a couple of hits too Cuba, c'mon.

Cuba. I ain't payin' for the sample—I ain't gonna pay you.

Jackie. I didn't snort that much?!!

Cuba. *(To TEDDY, referring to the album cover with the coke on it.)* Take that from him. *(Wipes dead roach off his shoe.)*

Jackie. I don't care.

Cuba. Take it from 'im.

JACKIE. It's bullshit.

CUBA. Don't be afraid. Grab the fucking thing. Grab the fuckin' thing. *(He snatches the album, hands it to TEDDY.)* Put it away from this guy. Get a card—

TEDDY. Yeah, yes.

CUBA. And put the stuff in the bag—this bag here.

TEDDY. This bag?

CUBA. Yeah. And don't ever be afraid. Where you don't do nothing.

JACKIE. Yeah, be a hard-on.

CUBA. *(Puts his suit over the back of a chair.)* You stand there, scared shitless, you don't move. Yer there with yer chest out, giving it up to the guy—you want 'im to stab you, yer so scared. You want this guy to stop ya from shittin' on yerself. I seen it in jail. A guy so scared when he got stabbed, he smiled...Yeah, he didn't shit on himself. You know why? He was dead. Tell 'im, Jackie.

JACKIE. Yeah.

CUBA. Tell 'im.

JACKIE. Yeah.

CUBA. *Yeah?*

JACKIE. *(to TEDDY)* That's it.

CUBA. A guy is bigger than you, you go get a baseball bat. You don't find a bat—

JACKIE. A broomstick, a mop handle, a garbage-can lid.

TEDDY. Anything.

JACKIE. Anything.

CUBA. You know who taught me that? Yer Grandmother.

TEDDY. Abuelita?

CUBA. *(to JACKIE)* Yeah, I swear. May she rest in peace.

JACKIE. What's that?

CUBA. What she did when I was a kid.

TEDDY. What was that, Pop?

CUBA. These kids beat me up—

TEDDY. Beat you up, really?

CUBA. I ran upstairs crying. I hid under my bed—

TEDDY. God, Pop.

CUBA. I didn't wanna come out. Your grandmother, okay, she made me come out and made me go back downstairs with her. *(using a child's voice)* No, I don't wanna go—no, don't make me go, please. The kids are down there—I'm afraid.

TEDDY. God, Pop.

CUBA. *(reflectively)* She made me go...She made me go down.

TEDDY. What happened then?

CUBA. She came down with me and we looked for the kids who beat the shit outta me.

TEDDY. Uh-huh.

CUBA. They were on Third Avenue—on the corner— playing skelzies. "That's them. They beat me up." She gave me this stick, this broom handle she brought down with her. Hold it, hold it, hold it tight, she says to me. You're gonna hit all of 'em. You're gonna hit 'em hard. "I don't wanna hit 'em—I'm afraid," I said to her. You don't hit 'em, I'm gonna hit you. *(pauses, recalling the moment)* She shoved me. Hit 'em. *(He grows angry.)* Hit 'em! Hit 'em! She kept shoving me. Hit him. She picked this guy out for me. Hit that guy—he's not looking—hit 'im. *(blurts out sharply)* I lifted that stick over my head—and I—BANG—BANG—BANG. Home runs. BANG—BANG—BANG. I hit every fucken one of 'em. *(He drops his hands to his sides, stands with his mouth gaped open, reliving the moment. He nods with an air of satisfaction, snapping his fingers.)* BANG—BANG—BANG! I did it. *(A disgusted smile slowly makes its way across his face.)*

TEDDY. And you never stopped doing it.

CUBA. What?!

TEDDY. *(shakes his head)* No. Nothing, Pop. *(pause)*

CUBA. *(referring to the coke and the plastic bag)* Finish doing that for me.

TEDDY. Okay.

CUBA. And when you finish, put it in the refrigerator—

CUBA. Yeah, put it in the...ah...in the bottle of vitamins.

TEDDY. All right. *(CUBA and JACKIE sit on the sofa.)*

CUBA. I don't like to hide nothing from him.

JACKIE. No—

CUBA. When I was shot in the bar—I realize.

JACKIE. No, that's good—

CUBA. I don't hide nothin'—*nothin'.* I ain't been around that much but when I'm here, he knows.

JACKIE. In case the cops come he knows—

CUBA. He knows what to do.

JACKIE. Yeah. But what I was saying was he knows where to go. Where to find it—you know. He grabs it and flushes it.

CUBA. Yeah. But I want him to know *why*—why I'm this shit.

JACKIE. He knows.

CUBA. He knows I'm in it to, ah, get by.

JACKIE. Whatta ya gonna do? Go on welfare?

CUBA. I rather rob a fucking bank! At least I can walk with my head *high*. Lemme tell ya something.

JACKIE. Tell me something.

CUBA. When my mother and me came over from Cuba—

JACKIE. Yeah.

CUBA. Back in...nineteen...forty-eight...forty-nine. We had *one* sandwich...one big superduper sandwich to last the ride. You know. *I'd* take a bite. *She'd* take a bite. Like that.

JACKIE. Yeah, right, so it can last youse longer.

CUBA. Yeah. But man, we were so hungry, we ate this monster sandwich my mother made—it was like this—

JACKIE. A foot long.

CUBA. *You* had to *see* it.

JACKIE. Yeah.

CUBA. Yeah. We ate it in four bites. She stood on one end of it—I stood at the other end—

JACKIE. Yeah—

CUBA. Yeah and we—

JACKIE. Demolished it.

CUBA. *Put it away.* Now we got nothin'—and we got South Carolina, North Carolina, Virginia, Washington— all these places to go till we got to New York.

JACKIE. Oh yeah.

CUBA. On the train was this soldier. If it wasn't for this soldier—man, God bless him. He gave my mother and me peanut-butter sandwiches. In those days they used to give the soldiers free peanut-butter sandwiches. Me and my mother ate peanut-butter sandwiches all they way here. *(pause)* I don't got much now. Cause you know I pissed it away.

JACKIE. Yeah, you and me both.

CUBA. But, I got one thing, got one thing. I gotta jar of peanut butter in the refrigerator.

JACKIE. Yeah?

CUBA. Yeah. Lemme show you.

TEDDY. I'll get it Pop.

CUBA. So you don't think I'm bullshittin' ya.

TEDDY. Look. *(holds out the jar)*

JACKIE. Yeah—I see it.

TEDDY. Remember, Pop?

CUBA. I hope to God I never have to open it.

JACKIE. Yeah—right.

TEDDY. Remember, Pop—you used to put peanut butter on my apples?

CUBA. Yeah.

TEDDY. When we used to watch the ball games.

CUBA. Uh-huh.

TEDDY. I used to put salt on his.

CUBA. When I had money, I used to dress 'im in *two-hundred-fifty-dollar* suits.

JACKIE. I remember.

CUBA. *two-hundred-fifty-dollar* suits—you remember?

JACKIE. Yeah.

TEDDY. I don't remember.

CUBA. You were a kid—a baby. Eight, nine. But you was the only kid walking around the Lower East Side in *two-hundred-fifty-dollar* suits.

TEDDY. Yeah?!

CUBA. Yeah.

JACKIE. Yeah.

CUBA. But I *fucked* myself up! Chasing his mother I lost a lot of jobs. When I was with her I had a *good* job working construction. One time I left the jobsite to go after his mother who went back to Puerto Rico. Connections—everything I lost running after his mother.

JACKIE. Pussywhipped.

CUBA. Nah, I wouldn't say that.

JACKIE. What else could it be.

CUBA. I loved her.

JACKIE. Well...hey, that's a whole 'nother story.

CUBA. Yeah.

JACKIE. *(meaning the cocaine)* You like that.

CUBA. It's *nice.*

JACKIE. It's on the money—that's what it is.

CUBA. I'm pretty sure this guy I'm bringin' it to is gonna like it.

JACKIE. Good, I like hearing that. We're gonna make money—good money.

CUBA. God willing.

JACKIE. Hope and pray, what else can you do.

CUBA. Money realizes yer dreams.

JACKIE. Mostly wet dreams...huh, Teddy?

CUBA. If you wanna jump offa the Empire State Building but you live up in the Bronx—

JACKIE. Or Brooklyn—where I live.

CUBA. If you ain't got money for your token, you better beg, borrow, or steal. And if yer old enough to beg, you're old enough to steal. So you end up what? You end up forgetting yer problems 'cause you got money in yer pockets—and you're living a life of crime.

JACKIE. That's the way it is.

CUBA. *(to TEDDY)* I want you to see that.

TEDDY. I understand.

CUBA. You know?

JACKIE. It's not pretty, but it's a living.

CUBA. A pretty shitty living.

TEDDY. Why jump from the Empire State Building, Pop?

JACKIE. Yeah Cuba, what's wrong with jumpin' off yer own building?

CUBA. Nothing. But if you're gonna go—go big! Off the top of the gorilla building. King-Kong style.

JACKIE. If it's good enough for King Kong—

CUBA. Yeah, right. That's right.

TEDDY. Monkey see, monkey do.

JACKIE. Nobody's original anymore, huh Teddy.

TEDDY. No.

CUBA. I'm happy. *(He puts on the gray pants of his suit.)*

JACKIE. Look at 'im. Look at yer father. You're gonna have to give 'im a hand. He can't zipper his pants. Tighten yer ass, Cuba—squeeze yer cheeks and hold your breath.

CUBA. Whattaya talkin'...It's my nuts. My nuts are too big.

JACKIE. You want me to tickle 'em for you—get 'em smaller.

CUBA. *(zippers his pants)* You see. The zipper was jammed.

JACKIE. Jammed on what, a pubic hair.

CUBA. A thread, you slob.

JACKIE. Sure, fatty.

CUBA. I'm fatty? You're fatty. *(to TEDDY)* Who's fatter? Who's fatter, him or me?

JACKIE. I got big bones.

CUBA. Yer full of shit.

JACKIE. That too.

CUBA. Lemme ask you something.

JACKIE. Don't ask me nothing.

CUBA. Yer bashful?

JACKIE. You're bashful.

CUBA. Admit yer fat.

JACKIE. I admit I do look a little heavy.

CUBA. You want me to admit I'm fat.

JACKIE. Admit it.

CUBA. I'll admit it if you tell me the truth about something.

JACKIE. The truth about what?

CUBA. About fat guys like you, you know, born fat, having little dicks.

JACKIE. *(explodes)* That's a myth!

CUBA. Relax, I was only askin'.

JACKIE. A myth. Everybody says that shit. That's pure and simple—

CUBA. *(jumping in)* Myth.

JACKIE. Shit.

CUBA. I'm only joking with you. You know I love you.

JACKIE. Yeah, you love me like a hard-on.

CUBA. Lemme kiss you to make it better.

JACKIE. Not on the lips. Kiss me here—on the head. *(CUBA kisses JACKIE on the top of his head.)*

CUBA. You feel better now?

JACKIE. You know something—I do, I feel better.

CUBA. Anything I can do for ya?

JACKIE. Yeah. I'll take a beer.

CUBA. That's a reasonable request. For a fat guy. *(Laughs out loud. Goes to the kitchen and opens the refrigerator. Spots JACKIE'S knapsack inside, picks it up.)* What's this?

JACKIE. That's mine. Oh, Jesus, I forgot.

CUBA. Whatta you walkin' around with yer lunch?

JACKIE. I got two pounds of pot in there. I almost forgot.

CUBA. From where?

JACKIE. This guy.

CUBA. With the coke?

JACKIE. These two pounds are his. He wants me to get rid of 'em for 'im.

CUBA. Just these two pounds?

JACKIE. By tomorrow night.

CUBA. Uh-huh.

JACKIE. I said I could.

CUBA. Yeah.

JACKIE. I can't. *(pause)* Do you know anybody—it's Columbian smoke.

CUBA. I dunno.

JACKIE. How come you don't know anybody?

CUBA. The people I got who come to me are people who only wanna buy coke. You know that.

JACKIE. I got the same problem. My people are strictly cokeheads. All I want is to give 'im his money. The rest, you know, whatever you sell this for, you keep.

CUBA. I don't know anybody, Jackie. I gotta think.

TEDDY. I know some, Pop.

CUBA. You what?

TEDDY. *(to JACKIE, picking up a cigarette)* You gotta light?

CUBA. Since when did you start smoking?

TEDDY. This year.

JACKIE. *(lighting TEDDY'S cigarette)* You know someone?

CUBA. How come I didn't see any cigarette butts around?

TEDDY. I don't smoke in the house.

CUBA. You inhale? *(TEDDY inhales and blows the smoke out.)*

JACKIE. Yeah.

TEDDY. Pop, you know who the guy is.

JACKIE. He'll buy the pot, this guy?

TEDDY. He gave you the bowler, remember, as a present?

CUBA. He gave me his Derby? That's the guy we're talking about?

TEDDY. Che.

CUBA. Yeah.

TEDDY. My friend, Che.

CUBA. He's the writer.

JACKIE. He's a writer, oh yeah?

TEDDY. He's the only Spanish writer—

CUBA. He's pretty famous, right?

TEDDY. *(nods yes)* He's the only Spanish writer—

CUBA. *(to TEDDY)* He shoots up shit? *(to JACKIE)* Yeah, he shoots up shit.

JACKIE. He's a junkie.

TEDDY. But he's the only Spanish writer—

CUBA. *(upset)* It's a shame, you know, a guy with all that talent pissing his life away. He looks like a bum.

TEDDY. But he's the only Spanish writer—

CUBA. A nice guy, but I only met him once.

TEDDY. *(quickly)* He's the only Spanish writer to win a Tony Award.

CUBA. You told me he wrote that play in the hospital, when he was in the hospital kicking that shit.

TEDDY. He wrote it the day after he got off heroin.

JACKIE. And he went back on it the day after that, when he made it big.

TEDDY. He's from around here.

CUBA. Yeah, he's from the Lower East Side.

JACKIE. Well, if this Mister Magoo is famous, he gotta have money.

CUBA. He's always broke, he sleeps in the park you told me.

JACKIE. Mister Magoo is a lowlife? Why you pulling my shirttail for?

TEDDY. No, he knows people. He knows the people who sell pot outta the social clubs around here.

JACKIE. That's nickel bag, I'm big time.

TEDDY. Yeah, but they sell. They sell a couple of pounds a night, everynight. Like the Beatles said: Everybody smokes pot.

CUBA. You smoke pot?

TEDDY. No.

CUBA. No what.

TEDDY. No I don't smoke pot.

CUBA. Swear.

TEDDY. Yeah, yes!

CUBA. Say it.

TEDDY. Say it?

CUBA. I swear I don't smoke pot.

TEDDY. C'mon, Pop, that's childish.

CUBA. Excuse me, that's what?

TEDDY. I swear I don't smoke pot.

CUBA. How come you don't smoke pot?

TEDDY. I don't that's all.

CUBA. You gotta have tried it. You try something to tell if you like it, or you don't like it.

TEDDY. I don't like it.

CUBA. Then you did try it?

TEDDY. No, I've smelled it when you've smoked it.

CUBA. I'm not gonna slap you—

JACKIE. C'mon, Cuba, he's a man.

CUBA. I'm gonna punch the shit outta you.

TEDDY. What did I do, Pop, huh?

CUBA. You wanna moke pot?

TEDDY. No, I don't wanna smoke pot.

CUBA. The day you wanna smoke pot—

TEDDY. Pop, I don't like the smell of pot.

CUBA. I know, I'm sayin'—

TEDDY. I know, Pop, but if I don't like the smell, I know I'm not gonna like smoking it.

CUBA. I'm sayin'...you come to me. You wanna smoke pot? You come to me, you say, Pop, I wanna smoke pot.

You don't go behind my back, that shit will piss me off. You understand?

TEDDY. Yeah, yes!

CUBA. You wanna do drugs?

TEDDY. No.

CUBA. No, I know, I'm sayin', you wanna do drugs, you do it with me, we do it together. You know what I'm sayin'?

TEDDY. Yeah, I know, yes.

CUBA. I rather have it that way, than the other way, you doing it with some asshole who don't give a fuck about you.

TEDDY. I understand.

CUBA. You wanna drink booze?

TEDDY. No, Pop.

CUBA. I know, I'm sayin'…you wanna drink? We get drunk. I'll get a bottle we drink it together. You wanna piece of ass?

JACKIE. I do.

CUBA. I'll get you a piece of ass. Some nice stink. Any kind of stink you want. White, black, Spanish, I'll get it for ya. A black chick is good for ya, bring you good luck.

JACKIE. Oh yeah? Like rubbing the tip of a black albino's prick.

CUBA. Jackie, I had sex with this black chick one time and the next day I hit the number. I swear to God. You understand what I been sayin' to you?

JACKIE. The old man loves you.

CUBA. What old man, fatty?

JACKIE. He don't wanna see you get hurt.

TEDDY. I know.

JACKIE. Whacha gonna do about the pot?

CUBA. Whatta 'bout this guy, Che?

JACKIE. Whatta 'bout him?

CUBA. He's a junkie.

JACKIE. Whatever you think.

CUBA. *(to TEDDY)* How'd you meet this guy?

TEDDY. We just happened to, you know, run into each other.

JACKIE and CUBA. Run into each other?

TEDDY. Yeah, yes!

CUBA. *(long pause, excited)* Whassamatter with you?!!

TEDDY. Nothing. I met 'im at St. Mark's Church, at a poetry reading.

JACKIE. You like poems? Ain't that something.

CUBA. This guy, yer learnin' anything from this guy, Che?

TEDDY. Yeah, I'm learning a lot from him, yes!

JACKIE. You write poems?

TEDDY. *(nods yes)* And prose.

JACKIE. What the hell is that?

TEDDY. It's ordinary language.

JACKIE. You read any of his things, Cuba?

CUBA. My reading ain't that good. I see him writing, you know, I thought he was doing his homework.

JACKIE. What kinda things you write about? You got any porno?

TEDDY. No.

CUBA. You been around this guy, Che, a lot?

TEDDY. Sometimes.

CUBA. Is he gonna get you somewhere, or something?

Teddy. I don't know.

Cuba. You dunno what?

Teddy. I don't know.

Cuba. He can't do nothing for you? He can't get you connections?

Teddy. He can do that.

Cuba. How come he don't do that for you?

Teddy. It's up to me.

Cuba. Up to you—what?

Teddy. To write something that is well written.

Cuba. Something like what?

Teddy. Like a play, a novel, a book of poems.

Jackie. Is that what you wanna be, a writer?

Cuba. He don't know what he wants to be. He's always thinking about nothing.

Jackie. Lemme see something you wrote?

Teddy. I don't have anything.

Jackie. I don't care what it is, I jus' wanna see if ya any good.

Teddy. No, I don't have—

Jackie. Lemme see—

Teddy. No!

Cuba. I dunno if I like you hangin' out with this guy, Che.

Teddy. How many of your friends have won a Tony Award? How many of your friends can even write their names?

Jackie. I can write my name.

Teddy. I didn't mean you.

Jackie. Gimme a pen and a piece of paper.

Cuba. He's a being a wiseass.

JACKIE. Gimme a pen and a piece of paper.

CUBA. Give him a pen and piece of paper, wiseguy.

TEDDY. *(hands JACKIE a pen and a piece of paper)* You don't have to do this.

JACKIE. Stay right here, don't move. Watch this. *(He writes his name.)*

TEDDY. *(takes the paper from JACKIE)* It's very nice.

JACKIE. Look at that penmanship.

TEDDY. It's very nice.

JACKIE. With that kinda penmanship I could be a secretary. Only I ain't got the legs for it. I perfected my penmanship in the joint, so I could be a legal secretary. Go 'head, Cuba, buddy, show him yours.

CUBA. I ain't got time for that.

TEDDY. I need my pen, Jackie.

JACKIE. It takes a second. Write yer name, Cuba.

TEDDY. He doesn't have to write his name.

JACKIE. Why not? I did. Go 'head, Cuba.

CUBA. Leave me alone.

JACKIE. What's the big deal?

CUBA. Yeah, what's the big deal?!

TEDDY. Can I have my pen, Jackie. Please.

JACKIE. Yer father is gonna write his name.

TEDDY. He doesn't want to.

JACKIE. Why not? What's the hassle with writing your name? I don't understand.

CUBA. Gimme the pen and the paper. *(Long pause as CUBA writes his name.)*

JACKIE. Lemme see it.

TEDDY. *(Snatches the paper out of his father's hand.)* I wanna see it first...Yeah, beautiful, it's better than yours, Jackie.

JACKIE. Oh, yeah? Lemme see...

TEDDY. *(rips the paper)* What did you say?

JACKIE. What the hell is going on?

TEDDY. Nothing.

CUBA. I can't write my name.

TEDDY. He can write it—

CUBA. I can write it—but you can't read it.

JACKIE. As long as you can—

CUBA. Forget it—awright? Do me the favor.

TEDDY. Pop, all I was trying to get across was...Che, is the only man, Latino, from the Lower East Side, with no education, to have been produced sucessfully, published with enthusiams, and is one of the well-known and re-spected artists around.

CUBA. The guy's a junkie. To me he's an asshole.

TEDDY. No, Pop, he's an accomplished individual.

CUBA. What?!

TEDDY. Pop, I don't want contribution to society to only be a nine-month future taxpayer. Monekys can have babies, that ain't so tough.

CUBA. What is it you want?

TEDDY. To be valued highly.

CUBA. To be what—

TEDDY. I dunno. Nothing.

CUBA. I don't understand this kid. I don't understand him. Hey?! I don't understand you.

JACKIE. Excuse me Cuba—is it gonna be a hassle doing business with Mister Magoo, what's his name, Che? Is it gonna bother you? I dunno, you know?

CUBA. *(to TEDDY)* You sure this guy knows the pot

dealers down in them social clubs?

TEDDY. Yeah, yes!

CUBA. I'm gonna go with you to see this guy, Che.

TEDDY. Yeah, yes.

CUBA. Awright?

TEDDY. No. It's better, Pop, if I go alone without you, and without the pot.

CUBA. And do what?

TEDDY. Locate Che.

JACKIE. You don't know if yer gonna find Mister Magoo?

TEDDY. I can find him, I just have to walk around. He's always in Tenth Street Park. Sometimes he stays with a girl who lives on Tenth and A—across from the park. The transaction can take place there. Simple.

CUBA. It ain't simple. If it was simple, that easy, there wouldn't be no laws against it.

TEDDY. Pop, what I'll do is get Che and the dealer he knows and bring them over to the girl's place, and then I'll call you from there.

CUBA. I don't want you there.

TEDDY. I'll be all right.

CUBA. Cops break in, no. You never know with this shift.

TEDDY. I wanna be there. Things go wrong or not, I wanna be there.

CUBA. Whatta hardhead. Why?

TEDDY. I think it's time, Pop, time you and me start seeing each other on this level. Other than father and son.

CUBA. But that's what we are, father and son. Whatta

you want?!

TEDDY. I wanna be there, I'm a man, Pop.

CUBA. How do you know this guy, Che, don't bring over one of those, you know, those beat artists?

TEDDY. No, Pop, Che wouldn't do that.

CUBA. One of these rip-off guys.

TEDDY. Che—would never do that.

CUBA. How do ya know?

TEDDY. Pop, I'm not a fool. I haven't lived with one arm tied behind my back.

CUBA. What's that supposed to mean?

TEDDY. Nothing.

JACKIE. But, you know, you gotta think, maybe, you know, there is that chance...the guy Mister Magoo is bringin' over is, you know, one of the bad guys.

CUBA. That's the way it is with this. You never never know.

JACKIE. In my time...when I was really in this, selling weight, you know? Not this penny-ante bullshit I'm dealing now, we went by yer word, yer word and and a handshake...And if you didn't keep yer word we gave you back yer hand. Yeah...Tell him, Cuba, tell him what it was like.

CUBA. He knows, he's not stupid, he reads.

JACKIE. But he wasn't there. You had to be there. Me and yer father—

TEDDY. Street-fighting men.

CUBA. He's smart.

JACKIE. You don't gotta tell me, I can see that.

TEDDY. We'll be doin' this together, Pop, like you said, to come to you, right?

CUBA. You really trust this guy?

TEDDY. I trust him.

CUBA. But do you really?

TEDDY. He's my friend.

CUBA. Yer friend...I'm a friend, and if I wasn't yer father, I'd say don't trust me!

JACKIE. Cuba? Whachu gonna give 'im for setting this all up? I mean if you let him do it.

CUBA. If I let 'im do it, I'm gonna give 'im everything.

JACKIE. Everything, Cuba?

CUBA. After you get your half, he gets the rest.

TEDDY. Shouldn't we split it?

CUBA. Yer gonna need the money to buy yerself a suit, something for yer graduation...for college...

(A loud knocking is heard on the apartment door.)

CUBA. Stay still. Don't move.

JACKIE. *(whispers loudly)* The cops?

(loud knocking)

CUBA. Hide the pot.

(loud knocking)

JACKIE. It sounds like the cops. Hide the pot.

CUBA. Where?

JACKIE. Stick it down yer pants, fatty, you won't know the difference.

(loud knocking)

TEDDY. Gimme, Pop, I'll put it behind the refrigerator. *(He does.)*

(loud knocking)

CUBA. *(upset, loudly)* Yeah, who is it?
REDLIGHTS. *(offstage, shouting)* Redlights. *(He laughs.)*
CUBA. Who?!
REDLIGHTS. *(offstage, shouting)* Redlights-Redlights-Redlights... *(He laughs.)* Redlights! *(CUBA opens the door slightly. He sticks his head in and shouts.)* Redlights!

(CUBA is startled. He opens the door. Standing in the doorway, laughing, grinning, with a cigarette propped in his mouth, is REDLIGHTS.)

CUBA. I thought it was the cops.

(LOURDES appearing and entering ahead of REDLIGHTS.)

LOURDES. Te lo dije, yo te lo dije, no? Que no tocara así. Boom. boom, eso asusta a cualquiera. *(REDLIGHTS winks at CUBA as he enters.)* Y Cuba, como tu 'ta? Te ve bien saludable. *(She smacks CUBA'S stomach.)*
[I told you, I told you, didn't I? Not to knock that way...that frightens people...And Cuba, how are you? You look very healthy.]
REDLIGHTS. Mira quien 'ta 'hi! Look who's here, mami. *(shaking JACKIE'S hand)* How's it hanging?...Long and

loose and full of juice. *(laughs)*

JACKIE. I can't complain.

REDLIGHTS. Good, I wasn't gonna lissen to ya if you did. You remember my bitch—jus' kiddin' baby. You remember my old lady, Lourdes.

LOURDES. *(To REDLIGHTS, looking at him while she shakes JACKIE'S hand.)* Una pata en el fundiyo—te voy a dar a ti.

[I'm going to give you a kick in the ass.]

JACKIE. *(shaking her hand)* A pleasure.

LOURDES. *(smiling at JACKIE)* Much gusto.

REDLIGHTS. *(warmly shakes CUBA'S hand)* Como esta, negro? *(doing an imitation of Ed Norton of The Honeymooners.)* Slip me five, so I'll know yer alive. *(He laughs.)* Kiss ya later I'm eatin' a potato. *(laughs)*

LOURDES. Déjalo, que hoy él está de película. Ese hombre, me tiene hasta aqui con esos jodios Honeymooners. Hay que déjalo. *(to REDLIGHTS, asking for coke)* Dame eso, papi. *(REDLIGHTS gives her a small vial.)* Puedo usar el baño, Cuba?

[Leave him alone 'cause today he's showing off. That man, I've had it up to here with those damn Honeymooners. You've got to drop it...Give me that, papi...Can I use the bathroom, Cuba?]

CUBA. Yeah, sure, the bathroom is through there. *(to TEDDY)* Show her.

TEDDY. It's over there.

LOURDES. Gracias. *(coming on to TEDDY)* Hay que lindo.

[How good-looking you are.] *(LOURDES exits with TEDDY through his room.)*

REDLIGHTS. Cubita, man, can you dig Norton of *The Honeymooners* going into a drugstore to get himself a box of prophylactics?...Can you dig that, Cubita, man? *(imitating Norton again)* Hello there...slip me five so I'll know yer alive. Yes, I would like to purchase a box of yer finest cigars, I mean— *(laughs like Norton) prophylactics. Preferably Trojans. Yes, sie, yes, sir! Lubricated of course. (Laughs. Using his own voice.)* Dig, you know how he does with his hands...He always goes like this...You know every time he's gonna do something, right, Cubita, you know, he does this... *(flings his hands out)* So I can dig 'im, you know, when he gets his scumbags, going like this... *(laughs)* before he puts one on. *(laughs)* The guy is a trip. *(LOURDES returns and resumes her place next to REDLIGHTS. To TEDDY.)* Mira pa' ya, quien e' ese, linguini? Qué pasa, qué lo tuyo, ha? De'pierta, and slip me five so I'll know yer alive. *(shakes TEDDY'S hand)*
[Look at that, who's this, linguini? What's happening, what's with you, ha? Wake up...]
   CUBA. *(to TEDDY)* You dunno who this is?
   REDLIGHTS. He knows me—everybody loves me.
   LOURDES. Deja te de la mierda, que ya eso apesta.
[Stop your shit, 'cause it stinks already.]
   CUBA. You don't remember him?
   REDLIGHTS. I remember you.
   CUBA. You don't remember him?
   REDLIGHTS. I remember you.
   TEDDY. No, I don't.
   CUBA. Look at 'im good.
   TEDDY. ...I don't.
   REDLIGHTS. Check out this face. *(He grins.)*

TEDDY. I'm sorry.

REDLIGHTS. You pissed on it. *(laughs)* Yeah, you pissed in my face.

TEDDY. I'm really sorry.

CUBA. You were a kid, a baby, you didn't know nothin'.

REDLIGHTS. I hope so. I hope he didn't know nothin'. You sure would hurt my feelin's if you had something personal against my face.

TEDDY. Yeah—

REDLIGHTS. *(jumps in immediately)* Yeah, yeah, you do?!!!

TEDDY. Nooo. Yeah, I understand. Yes!

REDLIGHTS. Forget it. It was my fault for sticking my nose where it didn't belong. *(to LOURDES)* Mami, lissen to this...They were changin' his diapers—I went over to look—

LOURDES. Oye! pero que tu eres aberiquo. Mirar pa' qué? Qué tu iba ver?
[Listen! but you're nosy. Look for what? What were you going to see?]

REDLIGHTS. His thing, awright, at his little tiny thing.

LOURDES. Ah! Como el tuyo.
[Ah! Like yours.]

REDLIGHTS. Bang! Zoom! So, Jackie, when I bent over the crib, I got it right between the eyes.

JACKIE. Bullseye.

CUBA. That's good luck.

JACKIE. Yer lucky yer mouth wasn't opened.

REDLIGHTS. I guess that makes us kinda like blood brothers. *(laughs, to LOURDES)* Mami, this is Cubita's son.

Check him out.

LOURDES. *(very sexy)* Ai! Como 'ta? Qué muneco, Cuba. hello. Somo estas?

[How are you? What a doll...How are you?]

TEDDY. Hi.

LOURDES. Dime una cosa, Cuba, él no se aparece e'paño, por qué?

[Tell me something, Cuba, he doesn't look Spanish, why?]

REDLIGHTS. Yeah, Cubita, dig it, he does look white.

CUBA. He looks like his mother.

LOURDES. Y tu mama? Dónde está?

[Your mother? Where is she?]

CUBA. She's in Puerto Rico.

TEDDY. My grandmother raised me.

REDLIGHTS. Hey, Cubita, huh, you gotta white boy, dig that. *(laughs)* That's good luck. I think.

CUBA. Whattaya want? He's American. He was born here. He ain't a spic—he's a gringo.

LOURDES. Pero, él es muy simpático.

[But he's very nice.]

CUBA. He's a good kid. Jus' thinks too much.

LOURDES. Tu entiende e'pañol?

[Do you understand Spanish?]

TEDDY. I understand it a little.

LOURDES. Pero tu no lo habla?

[But you don't speak it.]

TEDDY. No. I understand it better than I speak it.

REDLIGHTS. Mira, Cubita, dig this album, baby. When you hear this, you're gonna flip out. Where you put the album mami?

LOURDES. E'ta alli.
[It's there.]

REDLIGHTS. Get it. *(LOURDES hesitates.)* Avanza, hurry up? *(Reluctantly, LOURDES retrieves the album.)* Dig it, Cubita, e'ta heavy duty. E'te tipo is the daddy. The mane' un malote—he's bad. *(He reaches for the album, LOURDES drops it onto the floor. Picking it up.)* We play like that. Read it—you know who he is? *(JACKIE quickly crosses to CUBA to read the album cover for him.)*

JACKIE. "Recorded live at Sing Sing." Hey, that's where you was, Cuba.

CUBA. That's where we both were.

JACKIE. I was innocent—it was a bum rap.

REDLIGHTS. *(laughing, to CUBA)* Bum rap. They still say that shit? *(takes the album from JACKIE)* It's outta sight. Lemme hear one cut, awright, Cubita? E'ta caliente. *(REDLIGHTS goes to record player, starts to put album on. CUBA jumps up and motions him away from record player. CUBA puts album on, doesn't start player.)* Dynamite, baby. E'ta noche yo voy pa'l Corso, tu sabe? You know, a cosal, que se dice. Get down. *(He dances.)* A mete mano con el peso. Yeah, baby, me and the old lady are gonna go down to the Corso and I'm gonna throw some grease on the skillet and I'm gonna cook, baby. *(stops dancing, to TEDDY)* Linguini, lissen to this?

CUBA. He don't like Spanish music.

REDLIGHTS. No me diga...nah, no me diga eso.
[Don't tell me...don't tell me that.]

CUBA. I'm not shittin' yuh.

REDLIGHTS. De verdad?

CUBA. I swear.

REDLIGHTS. Why?

CUBA. He's a gringo.

TEDDY. I don't like it.

REDLIGHTS. That's like the Pope sayin' he hates being Catholic—but it's a living. Qué insulte—Dio' mio. *(to TEDDY)* Salsa, baby, salsa. It's in yer blood, linguini.

CUBA. He don't like rice and beans.

LOURDES. Oh, no, we gotta do something. Mira Cuba, traelo a mi casa. You'll like it the way I cook it.
[Look Cuba, bring him to my house...]

REDLIGHTS. Coño, man, that's our soul food. Yer breakin' my heart. Cubita, man, you sure he wasn't left on ya doorstep?

LOURDES. Y pasteles, te gusta pasteles?
[And "pasteles," you like "pastleles"?]

TEDDY. No. *(REDLIGHTS looks shocked.)*

LOURDES. Ah, ya yo sé, a ti te gu'ta el mafongo, verdad?
[Now I know, you like "mafongo," right?]

TEDDY. I hate it.

REDLIGHTS. He hates it?!! You know what hate means? Hate means you wish it didn't exist, that's what hate means. You hate it?! I'm gonna hit 'im—hold me back— I'm gonna let 'im have it. *(advances on TEDDY)*

LOURDES. No, no, no! He's only kidding.

REDLIGHTS. *(to CUBA)* I'm fuckin' with him, you know that. People, lissen to me. Lissen to me, people. No Spanish food in a spic can break his spirit. Right, Cubita?

CUBA. He's a gringo, I told ya awready. He was born here.

TEDDY. Excuse me. *(He starts for his room.)*
REDLIGHTS. Trebelin? Treviliqui—chill, papito, chill.
TEDDY. No, it's okay, excuse me.
REDLIGHTS. No-no-no-no. Commere-commere-commere.
LOURDES. Deja ese nene ya!
[Leave that boy alone now!]
REDLIGHTS. Commere!

(TEDDY returns and resumes his place. REDLIGHTS moves to record player to turn it on. CUBA dashes over, waves him away and turns on player. The music is a hot Latin salsa song.)

REDLIGHTS. Dig it. Dig it, papito, get into it. Botate. Pa'l piso, pa'l piso.
[Let loose. Take the floor, take the floor.]
TEDDY. No, I'll pass.
REDLIGHTS. *(urging TEDDY to dance)* Pa'l piso, pa'l piso.
TEDDY. No, sorry.
REDLIGHTS. *(to LOURDES)* Baila con él.
[Dance with him.]
TEDDY. No, I don't wanna dance.
LOURDES. Tu no quiere bailar conmigo?
[You don't want to dance with me?]
REDLIGHTS. Dance with her.
LOURDES. Vente. Nene. Déjame enseñarte unos pasitos. *(She grabs TEDDY'S hand.)*
[Come. Baby. Let me show you some little steps.]
REDLIGHTS. Pa'l piso, pa'l piso.
JACKIE. Go 'head, dance with her. Shake a leg.

REDLIGHTS. Metele mano.
[Dig her.] *(LOURDES dances by herself.)*
TEDDY. No, I don't wanna dance.
REDLIGHTS. You don't wanna dance to this kinda music?!
TEDDY. I don't like it.
REDLIGHTS. But if it was rock—you know, that metal an' shit—you'd get down.
CUBA. He don't know how to dance to Spanish music.
REDLIGHTS. Well he better learn.

(REDLIGHTS grabs LOURDES and they dance together fiercely. JACKIE rolls two joints of pot. REDLIGHTS dances with enthusiasm, growling with "yeahs" and "baya's." CUBA watches them with delight. TEDDY walks into his room, takes his writing pad and pen and sits on his bed. He begins to write. As the song plays, CUBA stands, cuts in on REDLIGHTS. JACKIE continues to roll the joints. REDLIGHTS dances by himself. TEDDY stops writing and covers his ears, then goes into CUBA'S room and slams the door. The music gently fades. CUBA, LOURDES and REDLIGHTS all sit. The two joints of marijuana are passed among them.)

REDLIGHTS. Cubita, man, you should come down with us on a Saturday night.
JACKIE. What do you think of that, pal?
REDLIGHTS. I think—I think—I think—I think.
LOURDES. E'ta nice. E'ta bien nice.
JACKIE. I got something better.
REDLIGHTS. I think.

JACKIE. You wanna buy a pound of pot?

CUBA. Jackie?

REDLIGHTS. I think—

JACKIE. Huh?

CUBA. Let's not talk about this—this is between you and me.

JACKIE. I'm not talking—I'm jus' saying: you wanna buy a pound?

REDLIGHTS. I think.

JACKIE. Don't fuck around. *(to LOURDES)* Excuse the language. *(to REDLIGHTS)* Don't fuck around. You wanna buy a pound?

CUBA. *(upset)* Let's not talk about this.

JACKIE. I'm not talkin', I'm jus' sayin': "You wanna buy a pound?"

REDLIGHTS. *(to CUBA)* Lo que yo vine a bu'car fué perico.
[What I came to look for was coke.]

JACKIE. Oh, I can get you something. If I get you the coke, Whatta 'bout the pot?

CUBA. *(angry)* You don't lissen, huh? Whatta you doin'?!!

JACKIE. Talkin'. *(to REDLIGHTS)* I might have coke. *(to CUBA)* I'm not sayin' anythin'.

REDLIGHTS. Do' gramo'.

LOURDES. Tres, papi.

JACKIE. *(nods in understanding)* I can get you something in the vicinity of two grams...one-and-a-half...a gram-...half a gram... *(quickly, to REDLIGHTS)* But if I do that, whatta 'bout the pot?

CUBA. *(exploding)* Whacha doin'? Whatta you doin'?

(slowly for effect) What are you doing?

JACKIE. Talkin'.

REDLIGHTS. Ahora tu sabe?

JACKIE. You want the coke now, yeah. *(to CUBA)* I'm not sayin' nothin'. *(to REDLIGHTS)* Maybe I can get you a little. *(to CUBA)* That's all. *(to REDLIGHTS)* But if I do...whatta 'bout the pot?!

CUBA. *(angry)* Get out! Get out. I mean it...get out.

JACKIE. I'm not talkin'.

CUBA. Good-bye.

JACKIE. I'm jus' sayin'. *(to REDLIGHTS)* You interested?

REDLIGHTS. No.

JACKIE. Why you wastin' my time for?

REDLIGHTS. I want coke.

JACKIE. I got pot.

CUBA. Jackie, hey, let's go. You got pot where? Where you got pot? You got pot nowhere. I got pot. I'm handling it.

JACKIE. I was jus' sayin', there's pot, you interested? I wasn't talkin'.

REDLIGHTS. I understand, Cubita.

CUBA. It pisses me off when everybody knows what I'm doin'. *(smiles at LOURDES)* I don't mean nothin'.

REDLIGHTS. You gotta be that way, Cubita.

CUBA. I gotta be that way. You know how many times I changed my phone number? I don't even know my phone number. What's my phone number? I'm not that way, everybody knows how much shit I'm selling. An' before you know I gotta junkie ripping me off and I don't wanna kill nobody.

JACKIE. You ain't gonna kill nobody. I wasn't talkin'—I was jus' sayin'.

CUBA. Good-bye, Jackie. *(to REDLIGHTS)* Get him outta here before I kill 'im. *(LOURDES ad-libs good-byes.)* My door is open. When you wanna come up—come up. But, you know, stay awhile.

LOURDES. Un momentito... *(crosses to TEDDY)*

CUBA. Redlights, Tu entiendes? Verdad? What I'm saying?

REDLIGHTS. Yeah, man. Así son las cosa'.
[That's the way it is.]

CUBA. Yeah, así son.

LOURDES. Teddy...take care, nene. *(crosses to door)*

REDLIGHTS. I knew you were gonna dig that suit. Pierre Cardin?

CUBA. Yeah, these are the pants.

REDLIGHTS. Those are them? It looks nice. You know I lifted it from Barneys.

CUBA. Barney's? Keep up the good work. *(RED-LIGHTS, LOURDES and CUBA ad-lib good-byes. RED-LIGHTS and LOURDES exit.)*

JACKIE. See ya, buddy, okay?

CUBA. You gotta big friggin' mouth.

JACKIE. I know, I'm sorry, yeah.

CUBA. You want things too fast.

JACKIE. I know, I'm sorry, yeah.

CUBA. Yeah.

JACKIE. Yeah. *(CUBA gently pushes JACKIE out and closes the door.)*

(He bangs on the door from offstage.)

JACKIE. You're not mad at me, huh, Cuba?

(No response from CUBA. He bangs on the door again.)

CUBA. Be good to yerself.
JACKIE. *(off)* I'm sorry, Cuba, awright?
CUBA. Yeah.
JACKIE. *(off)* Yeah, we're sorry? Or, yeah, buy yerself a pretzel, Jackie, and jump off the Brooklyn Bridge!
CUBA. Yeah, I'll see you tomorrow.

(JACKIE, off, bangs on the door.)

JACKIE. See you, Cuba, buddy. *(CUBA carefully cleans up the apartment.)*
CUBA. Teddy?
TEDDY. *(from his room)* Pop?...What, Pop?
CUBA. Do me a favor.
TEDDY. What?
CUBA. Get me a clean shirt.
TEDDY. A clean shirt?
CUBA. Get me a white one.
TEDDY. Awright.
CUBA. Please, awright?

(TEDDY enters the living room with the white shirt.)

CUBA. Lookit you.
TEDDY. What?
CUBA. When yer gonna fix that hair? You look like...I don't know whachu look like. Gimme yer comb. *(TEDDY*

hands him his comb.) Comb yer hair. *(He hands the comb back to TEDDY.)*

TEDDY. For what, Pop? I'm not going anywhere.

CUBA. For yerself. You dunno the way you look is the way people treat you? You look like shit. Yer gonna be treated like shit. Don't you got any shoes?

TEDDY. I gotta pair.

CUBA. One pair of shoes?

TEDDY. They're in good condition.

CUBA. *(puts on his shirt)* That's because you don't wear 'em, yer in them shitty sneakers all the time, I'm gonna throw them out.

TEDDY. No, Pop, c'mon.

CUBA. I'm gonna have to start making some real money. Get you some clothes, shoes, you need 'em. I'm embarrassed awready—looking at you. Shoes are the most important thing on a man.

TEDDY. Really?

CUBA. You can look like nothin', but if ya gotta pair of nice-looking shoes on, yer something. There's a difference, a big difference. You wanna do somethin' for me?

TEDDY. Like what?

CUBA. Like, you know, pass a quick iron over this shirt—no big thing.

TEDDY. I'll do it.

CUBA. You wanna do it?

TEDDY. I'll do it Pop.

CUBA. You ain't doing nothin', right?

TEDDY. I'll do it.

CUBA. You ain't busy.

TEDDY. No.

CUBA. Huh?

TEDDY. I'll do it.

CUBA. Just—you know, a *one-two*, that's that. Do that for me.

TEDDY. I'll do it Pop. It's done. *(TEDDY goes to the kitchen, gets out the ironing board and the iron and brings them in the living room. He proceeds to iron his father's shirt. CUBA walks upstage to the statue of the Virgin.)*

CUBA. You see the bottle of Agua Florida?

TEDDY. No. *(CUBA exits to the bathroom, reenters with the Agua Florida and crosses back to the statue. He pours a handful of the cologne, splashes it on his face, runs his fingers through his hair, massages the back of his neck. Repeats the action.)* How come you do that?

CUBA. It makes me feel better. It takes all the negative shit outta me. It goes with these... *(TEDDY watches as CUBA takes three necklaces of colorful beads from around the neck of the statue of the Virgina Mary, one by one. He kisses the beads and makes the sign of the cross. He repeats this action two more times. He hangs the beads around his own neck and tucks them under his T-shirt.)*

TEDDY. What do they do? Are they supposed to do something, like ward off evil? You know, if you don't wanna be bitten by Dracula you wear garlic around your neck.

CUBA. No, this is serious, with this you don't fool around. Whatta you know about this?

TEDDY. Nothing, Pop.

CUBA. You didn't touch these?

TEDDY. Those?

CUBA. My "coyales" yeah.

TEDDY. No. *(CUBA proceeds to fill a shot glass with dark Bar-cardi rum. He places it in from of La Caridad del Cobre.)* But what if I did?

CUBA. This is serious. You don't touch them.

TEDDY. Why can't I touch them, or wear them?

CUBA. E'tan reglao.

TEDDY. What does that mean?

CUBA. Fixed...They been worked. Prepared. Made especially for me. You finish with that shirt?

TEDDY. Yes, here. *(Walks over to CUBA and hands him his shirt.)* Is that like "santeria"? Spiritualism.

CUBA. I dunno. "Las Siete Potencias" is what I call it.

TEDDY. "La Siete Potencias," ha?

CUBA. The Seven Afro-Cuban Powers. Yeah, she's one of them—*(He points to the statue.)* La Caridad del Cobre. *(He starts putting on his shirt.)*

TEDDY. Why is she dark skin? 'Cause in school, when I was in Mary Help of Christians, she was white.

CUBA. I dunno.

TEDDY. *(looks at the statue)* She's prettier. She got large black eyes, a nice head of reddish-brown hair, beautiful full lips. If Hugh Hefner was here, I bet he'd make her a Playboy Centerfold.

CUBA. Don't mess around with that.

TEDDY. I'm only kidding, Pop. I'm just making a joke.

CUBA. How's this shirt look?

TEDDY. Nice. How did you like the way I pressed it?

CUBA. Terrific. You got talent. You can work in a Chinese laundry.

TEDDY. 'Buelita was always into the saints.

CUBA. Your grandmother, she lived pa' lo' santo'...

TEDDY. Really.

CUBA. She was the one who paid for coyales.

TEDDY. A lot?

CUBA. Yeah.

TEDDY. How much did they cost?

CUBA. A lot.

TEDDY. Did you pick out the color of the beads you wanted to wear?

CUBA. *(putting his tie on)* What is this, a fashion show, whatta you think?

TEDDY. I dunno, that's why I'm asking. When 'Buelita was alive last year you weren't around that much. That's why I'm asking you.

CUBA. Every saint gotta color.

TEDDY. Your beads are yellow.

CUBA. My beads are yellow. La Caridad del Cobre, yellow is her color. San Lazaro—

TEDDY. Saint Lazarus—

CUBA. He got his color. You make a promise to him, the beads gotta be his color.

TEDDY. I see. *(pause)* What promise did you make?- ...Huh, Pop?

CUBA. I don't wanna talk about it.

TEDDY. C'mon, Pop.

CUBA. I don't wanna talk about it.

TEDDY. C'mon, Pop, I just wanna know.

CUBA. Tomorrow.

TEDDY. Did you have to make a promise?

CUBA. Tomorrow. It's supposed to rain. Tomorrow we'll talk.

TEDDY. You had to.

CUBA. Yeah, I hadda.

TEDDY. You hadda, uh-huh.

CUBA. *(laughs to himself)* What do you want to know? Yer grandmother took me to this lady.

TEDDY. What lady?

CUBA. Doña something. I forgot her name, she's an e'periti'ta in Brooklyn. She told me you gotta do this and you gotta do that. *(He crosses to the fridge for coke and snorts a bit through the following, while packing the coke sample to take with him.)*

TEDDY. In order to do what?

CUBA. In order to stay outta jail, that's what.

TEDDY. I don't understand.

CUBA. Me and these five Italian guys gave some shit over to this guy, a narc.

TEDDY. You didn't know he was a Fed?

CUBA. No, he was a Puerto Rican guy—

TEDDY. A Latino.

CUBA. What Latino? He was Puerto Rican. A nice guy, he didn't wanna bust me, he liked me. But what could he do, he pinched all of us, it's his job. A good job too. I like to see you become something like that, a Fed. They gotta very good pension.

TEDDY. I'll think about it. What happened next? What happened next?

CUBA. Yer grandmother bailed me out.

TEDDY. ...And?

CUBA. My lawyer told me, I was gonna do a lot of time, I sold to a Fed. Yer grandmother, she took me to see the e'periti'ta.

TEDDY. The lady in Brooklyn?

CUBA. Outta all the people who were there since six in the morning, she took me ahead of all of 'em. Yer grandmother says to her: "My son is going to jail for a long time. Can you help him?" She said, yeah—but only if I believe.

TEDDY. Believe in her?

CUBA. In...you know, santeria. I said, yeah, I believe in it. What do I gotta do? I'll do anything.

TEDDY. What did you have to do?

CUBA. *(snorts)* Promise to become a saint. Give my head to the Virgin Mary.

TEDDY. You had to become a saint?

CUBA. Yeah.

TEDDY. God, Pop...Are those those people who always wear white, and the women wear handkerchiefs on their heads?

CUBA. Yeah.

TEDDY. You were supposed to be one of those?

CUBA. Yeah.

TEDDY. Devote yourself to God and the saints?

CUBA. How many times, yeah! And pay her fifteen hundred dollars. How's my hair?

TEDDY. Fifteen hundred dollars? Gimme the comb. *(He combs his father's hair.)*

CUBA. She washed my hair with leaves—

TEDDY. Bend down. Leaves? *(combs the back of CUBA'S hair.)*

CUBA. Leaves, yeah, and praying—

TEDDY. Uh-huh.

CUBA. She gave me a bath too.

TEDDY. She bathe you? Turn your head to the side.

CUBA. No. She filled the bathtub, I got in, she came over and said, say a Hail Mary. I don't know what it was—but when I was saying the Hail Mary, she put this green liquid over my head—

TEDDY. Finish. What else?

CUBA. I finish. She said, we're finish, get dress. I'm gonna give you something. The necklace, my beads. I kissed them. She told me to kneel down, kneel down in front of La Caridad del Cobre, and promise I'll keep my word to her. I promise, I said to the statue, I give you my head, take it. Jus' as I was about to go, la e'periti'ta went into, like a trance. She started shuddering. *(He demonstrates.)* It scared the shit outta me. Then she gave me this powder. When the judge is gonna sentence you, she said, you bring it up to yer lips and blow it. Blow it hard. And you don't do it before, you don't do it after, you, you do it—

TEDDY. Right at that moment.

CUBA. Right at that moment, yeah. The judge says, all rise. I said, where's the powder. On the count of first-degree possession with the intention of distribution—*(slowly for effect)* I find—Anthony Vito, guilty. Richard Carlo, guilty. Rossi, guilty. Peppino, guilty. Tommy something, guilty. Joseph Cuba...I find—I went like this, real fast—I find you—I blew it— *(He blows.)* not guilty. Gimme my jacket.

TEDDY. *(hands CUBA his jacket)* Did you try to keep

your promise?

CUBA. What good's a promise if it ain't on a piece of paper.

TEDDY. You didn't keep your word to the Virgin Mary?

CUBA. I had business, business. Bills, lawyers, yer grandmother to take care of. You.

TEDDY. Nothing happened to you for not keeping yer promise?

CUBA. I'm not happy. I'll never be happy.

TEDDY. Selling drugs?

CUBA. Whattaya mean?

TEDDY. You won't be happy.

CUBA. No.

TEDDY. Selling drugs—it's hard to be happy.

CUBA. Making money, making money, it's hard to make money. I ain't gonna make the money I made because of this.

TEDDY. I don't understand.

CUBA. I made a lot of money sellin' drugs, right? I promised God, and everybody up there, you know, I'm not gonna sell drugs. I didn't keep my promise—I'm still selling drugs but I ain't making any money.

TEDDY. And that's what you get for not keeping your promise?

CUBA. Yeah...this kinda thing comes back on yer kid, or it falls on somebody you love. You, yer okay. You ain't blind, you ain't crippled, yer okay, thank God. So, it's gotta be on me. I ain't happy. But I'm alive.

TEDDY. Retribution.

CUBA. What's that?

TEDDY. What you said, Pop.

CUBA. Say it again.

TEDDY. Retribution.

CUBA. I dunno what that is. What is it??

TEDDY. You sell drugs. *(Long pause. No response from CUBA.)* Pop?

CUBA. I'm here.

TEDDY. Did you hear me? *(No response from CUBA.)* You sell drugs?

CUBA. *(upset)* Yeah, I sell drugs, I heard you.

TEDDY. I'm sorry.

CUBA. Yer sorry for what? I'm the one selling drugs.

TEDDY. It's evil.

CUBA. Yeah, it's evil.

TEDDY. You been dealing—

CUBA. Yeah.

TEDDY. You been dealing in the corruption—

CUBA. Yeah.

TEDDY. —and in the destruction of lives.

CUBA. Yeah.

TEDDY. It's evil.

CUBA. Yeah, I said it's evil, it's evil. Whaddaya sayin'?

TEDDY. You're dealing death. *(pause)* It's only right you suffer—or, you see someone you love very much suffer for what you have done. *(pause)* Pop?

CUBA. *(incredulous)* What I done? What I done? I kept you alive sellin' drugs. Yer alive today 'cause of drugs. You owe yer life to the drugs I sold. The drugs I sold put food in yer mouth, gave you a warm bed, money in yer pocket so you don't feel like shit. Who the hell you think you are? What I done. When you were in the hospital—you had trouble with yer legs—who took care of that? God? Nooo. *Drugs!* I took care of that, sellin' shit on the street. And lemme tell ya somethin' else. Don't go giving me these big words 'cause sometimes...I know what they mean. Where the fuck are my keys? You got some pair balls. What I done! I was shot in a bar—

TEDDY. Six times in the bar.

CUBA. *(Points to parts of his body.)* Here, here, here, here, here, here...What I done, right, for you!

TEDDY. *(guiltily)* Yeah.

CUBA. *What?*

TEDDY. Yes!

CUBA. Yer really pissin' me off. Don't go against me.

TEDDY. I'm not taking sides against you, Pop.

CUBA. Lissen, you bring this guy here, I ain't going nowhere.

TEDDY. What guy, Che?

CUBA. You tell him to bring the dealer over here with him.

TEDDY. We're not gonna go over there?

CUBA. No, they're gonna come to me. Anything funny happens I want it to happen here, where I got the edge.

TEDDY. Nothing is gonna happen, Pop.

CUBA. How long you been selling drugs to tell me about my business? Who are you? Yer nothin' but a piece of shit when it comes to drugs. *(immediately says:)* Gimme a kiss, commere.

TEDDY. *(upset)* Yeah.

CUBA. Don't say it like that.

TEDDY. Don't say—

CUBA. Yeah. Like—yeah, if I have to, I'll kiss you. You don't wanna kiss me? Fuck you. Fix this place up a little, for me. Put the board back where it goes. *(Finds his keys on top of the refrigerator.)* Don't forget to get ahold of this guy— for Jackie.

TEDDY. Che. No, I won't. What time do you want him here?

CUBA. Tomorrow night.

TEDDY. Is that when yer coming home?

CUBA. *(knocks over an ashtray)* Get that for me. Yeah, I'll be home tomorrow night. Do me a favor, check the ashtrays, make sure there's no pot in them. Wash the ashtrays— it stinks up the house, I can't sleep smellin' that shit.

TEDDY. I see you tomorrow.

CUBA. Okay?

TEDDY. Yes, I'll do it.

CUBA. Be a good boy. Lock the door behind me. *(He exits. TEDDY locks the door. He stares down at the fallen ashtray for a moment. He crosses to the sofa and sits. Silence. He springs to his feet. Rushes into his room where he lifts his mattress, and removes a small brown paper bag. He rushes back into the living room, dumps the contents of bag onto the coffee table. We see a hypodermic syringe, a bottle cap and a ten-dollar bag of heroin. He rushes into the kitchen to get a cup of water and matches. Returning to the living room, he sits on the sofa and prepares a shot of heroin for himself. He opens the heroin bag, empties the contents into the bottle cap.)*

TEDDY. *(Using the syringe to withdraw water from the cup.)* I wonder how much water to put in for one bag?...I dunno, I forgot. *(He tries to inject the heroin into his arm.)* I dunno...I dunno how...I need Che. I can't do this to myself. If Che was here, he'd do it for me. *(He looks out at the audience.)*

Blackout

END OF ACT I

ACT II

Early morning the next day. The apartment is neat, orderly. JACKIE is sprawled out on the living-room sofa, asleep. His legs are up on the coffee table, his head rests against the back of the sofa, his pants are visibly opened.

CUBA is alone in TEDDY'S room. He is searching through his son's clothing, looks inside TEDDY'S shoes. Hunting for a more telling insight into his son's privacy, he eyes a pair of TEDDY'S jockey shorts. He takes the shorts and brings them up to the light, critically examines them. He moves over to TEDDY'S bed, looks in his writing pad, attempts to read what TEDDY has written. Defeated, he slams the book down. He looks under the bed. He is moving to lift up the mattress when TEDDY appears in the doorway to the apartment.

TEDDY. Pop?
CUBA. Teddy?
TEDDY. *(asking for his blessing)* 'Cion.
CUBA. Dio' te bendiga.
[God bless you.] *(TEDDY bolts the apartment door.)*
TEDDY. *(approaches CUBA, concerned)* What are you look-ing for, Pop?
CUBA. Where'd you go?

TEDDY. For what?

CUBA. For what?! Whaddaya mean, for what? I wanna know where'd you go?

TEDDY. No, Pop, for what—particular thing were you looking for?

CUBA. Where'd you go?

TEDDY. To look for Che. I went to tell him to come here.

CUBA. How 'bout the guy?

TEDDY. He's coming over with the pot dealer—he went to get him, to pick him up. Did you jus' get home?

CUBA. (opens the refrigerator) Did you eat?

TEDDY. Yeah, yes.

CUBA. (looks at TEDDY) You look like you ate nothin'.

TEDDY. I ate.

CUBA. You look pale. (He looks into TEDDY'S eyes. He opens TEDDY'S eyes wide with his fingers. He steps back and glares at him.) Whassamatter with you?

TEDDY. Nothing's wrong with me.

CUBA. You feel awright?

TEDDY. You want me to swear?

CUBA. Swear.

TEDDY. I feel fine.

CUBA. Something I should know?

TEDDY. No.

CUBA. No!

TEDDY. No.

CUBA. Are you happy?

TEDDY. I dunno, Pop.

CUBA. What's to know about being happy? Yer happy or yer not happy.

TEDDY. I'm happy.

CUBA. How happy?

TEDDY. A little.

CUBA. A little happy, yer a little happy—so there's gotta be something, yer only a little happy. You gotta be happier. I know yer keeping something from me. That's not nice. If I can't help you, nobody can. You know when ya doin' somethin' stupid.

TEDDY. Don't worry.

CUBA. I don't like you spending too much time with this guy.

TEDDY. What guy, Pop?

CUBA. You know what guy.

TEDDY. I know.

CUBA. Che.

TEDDY. You remember his name when you want to.

CUBA. A dope fiend is always after one thing—more shit to shoot in his vein.

TEDDY. Yes, most are—but Che is not a dope fiend.

CUBA. *(shocked)* Excuse me. This guy is not what?

TEDDY. He's a addict.

CUBA. The same shit.

TEDDY. No, Pop, he's a human being.

CUBA. It's the same shit from any angle.

TEDDY. I don't know.

CUBA. I'm tellin' you.

TEDDY. What?

CUBA. Same shit.

TEDDY. Pop...a dope fiend is the lowest, most vile—a fiend will sell his mother for a shot of heroin.

CUBA. You tellin' me about drugs? Look who's tellin' me about drugs.

TEDDY. I'm tellin' you about human beings.

CUBA. Lissen to this shit. *(to JACKIE)* Yer lissening to this?

JACKIE. *(walking up)* Wha'? What? Cucarachas? *(He closes his eyes again.)*

CUBA. Go back to sleep.

TEDDY. An addict is a human being with a sickness.

CUBA. How do you know?

TEDDY. He's a human being, trapped, with a chemical need.

CUBA. I'm a human being.

TEDDY. Yes. I know.

CUBA. You know too much.

TEDDY. I'm only voicing my opinion, Pop, nothin' else.

CUBA. Be careful with me.

TEDDY. Pop, I know more than you think.

JACKIE. That's nice, I like hearin' that.

CUBA. Whaddaya sayin' with that?

TEDDY. ...Che is special. Che did time. Che—

CUBA. *I* done time...I was *shot*—dragged outta the bar—they closed the fucken bar, left me on the sidewalk, on top of spit, and bird shit, with six fucken bullet holes in me and yer tellin' me he's special? No, *I'm* special.

TEDDY. Yes.

CUBA. Somethin's goin' on here. I can see it in your eyes.

TEDDY. Nothing, Pop.

CUBA. Bullshit!

JACKIE. Easy, Cuba.

CUBA. Bullshit! Special. I'm special.

TEDDY. What do you want from me, Pop.

CUBA. What's inside yer head, right now...Tell me.

TEDDY. Pop—

CUBA. Say it! Say it to me!

TEDDY. Ideas...

CUBA. What kinda ideas?

TEDDY. My own.

CUBA. No.

TEDDY. I'm lying?

CUBA. Who's been puttin' funny ideas in yer head?

TEDDY. No one.

CUBA. *No.*

JACKIE. Not me.

TEDDY. No?

CUBA. Che.

TEDDY. I have a mind.

CUBA. Che.

TEDDY. I have my own mind.

CUBA. Look at me.

TEDDY. I don't wanna look at you, now.

CUBA. I'm askin' you. Look at me.

TEDDY. Right now, no, I don't want to.

CUBA. *(slowly for effect)* Look at me.

TEDDY. I'm looking at you.

JACKIE. Cuba always gets his way.

CUBA. No. I don't always get my way. *(To, TEDDY, slowly for effect.)* Look at me.

TEDDY. Yes.

CUBA. *(with great force)* Whadda you wanna be, like Che?! A junkie!

TEDDY. *(angry)* No, I wanna be like you, a drug dealer!

(Loud knocking is heard.)

CUBA. *(angry)* Yeah?!

CHE. *(offstage)* City morgue, you kill 'em, we chill 'em.

JACKIE. What the frig is that?

TEDDY. It's Che.

CUBA. *(upset)* Who is it?

CHE. *(off)* Mister Marvelous.

TEDDY. Pop, it's Che.

CUBA. Tell him to wait.

TEDDY. You're not gonna let him in?

CUBA. What did I say to you?

TEDDY. To wait.

CUBA. Let him wait. *(He walks over to the statue of La Caridad del Cobre.)*

TEDDY. Che?

CHE. *(off)* I'm here.

TEDDY. Wait, okay?

CHE. *(off)* I ain't goin' any place. *(CUBA tilts the statue forward and reaches underneath it, withdraws a small-caliber handgun in a holster, which he clips onto the waistband of his pants.)*

JACKIE. I don't like what I see.

TEDDY. *(frightened)* Pop?

CUBA. *(adjusts the gun)* Let 'im in.
JACKIE. I don't like what I see, Cuba.
TEDDY. Pop, no.
JACKIE. Whachu doing, Cuba?
CUBA. Let 'im in.
JACKIE. Lemme know, Cuba, whacha gonna do?
TEDDY. Pop, please.
CUBA. Let this guy in.
TEDDY. C',mon, Pop, put that away, please.
JACKIE. I ain't gonna jus' stand here, whahhaya gonna do, lemme know.
CUBA. Get out the fucking way.
TEDDY. No, Pop, I'll let him in.
JACKIE. I'm gonna let him in.

(From off, loud knocking.)

CHE. Let me in.
CUBA. Let him in.
JACKIE. Let me let him in.
TEDDY. *(rushes past JACKIE)* I'm gonna let him in.
JACKIE. *(to CUBA)* And what are you gonna do? *(No response from CUBA.)* Stay like that. I like you jus' like that. Calm. Like me, always calm. Leave the dramatics to Mickey Rooney.

(Loud knocking. CUBA stands in the living room, tight, serious. TEDDY opens the door. CHE enters. He is wearing a wide-brimmed fedora and what appears to be a zoot suit: broad-shouldered, baggy yellow coat draping below his knees, flared purple pants cuffed skintight around the ankles above oversized

waxed shoes. He strikes the "Pachuco" pose, swinging a long keychain in a circle.)

CHE. *(To CUBA, using a Chicano accent.)* Hey, big gabacho macho, you wanna buy a zoot, a tacuche? I give you this one, ese. First-class hepcat trapos. Lemme tell you, ese, the bato knows how to swing, swing, ese.

TEDDY. *(Tense, caught in the middle, quickly looks at CHE and then at his father.)* You remember each other, right? *(CHE extends his hand to CUBA. CUBA shakes CHE'S hand reluctantly.)*

CHE. Ese... *(He holds CUBA'S hand tightly, does not release it. It is obvious CUBA is annoyed by this.)* Anybody bother you, this bato will beat the sucker black and blue...comprende, ese? *(Releases CUBA'S hand, breaks up laughing. Using his natural voice.)* You remember me, right, man? *(No response from CUBA, who glares at CHE.)*

TEDDY. He remembers you, Che.

CHE. He looks like he don't wanna remember me. *(to CUBA)* I'm gonna hug you anyway. *(He hugs CUBA warmly. CUBA remains tight, distant.)* ...I felt that. You gotta piece on you.

TEDDY. No, he doesn't. *(CHE reaches for CUBA'S side. CUBA smacks his hand away.)*

CHE. *(to TEDDY)* Oh, no? Okay. If you say he ain't gotta gun on 'im, he ain't gotta gun on 'im. But if Cuba says he ain't gotta gun on 'im, I'm gonna start to worry.

CUBA. I gotta gun.

CHE. Now we know where we stand. One of us is armed. I ain't gotta piece on me. *(opens his jacket)* Yer welcome to check. *(to JACKIE)* You wanna frisk me? *(JACKIE gives him a hard stare.)* You gotta piece on you too? *(No response from JACKIE.)* You look like the type who never steps outta the house without one. *(awkward silence)* Well, it's good to see you, Cuba. I know...it's the way I'm dressed, you don't like the vines, that's cool, yer entitled. *(to TEDDY)* How you like me as a Pachuco?

TEDDY. Great.

CHE. *(using a Chicano accent again)* Jefe. a bato loco, a street-cruisin' dude.

TEDDY. Why are you dressed like that?

CHE. *(drops the accent)* I'm bored—bored with myself.

TEDDY. Where did you get the clothes?

CHE. In California, when I was working on *T.J. Hooker.*

TEDDY. You worked on *T.J. Hooker?*

CHE. Yeah, man, I was one of the writers.

TEDDY. Siddown.

CHE. *(takes a seat on the sofa)* Nice sofa. Comfortable. Feels lived in. Like me.

TEDDY. It's old.

CHE. How old?

TEDDY. Very old.

CHE. I love old things. Old people. *(looks at CUBA and at JACKIE, continues)* Old sayings. Old money. Old values. Old fossils. Like Cuba. Whassamatter Cuba? Smile. It's a beautiful world. Lemme see yer best thighs-and-hips smiles? *(He smiles broadly. To JACKIE.)* I love yer socks. I admire men who wear black nylon socks with white sneakers. They're a rare breed. It's wonderful. I always related the hairy legs, the black nylon socks, and the white sneakers with masculinity. Yer Italian, or yer from Brooklyn, or crazy! Jus' kiddin' with you. *(No response from JACKIE.)*

TEDDY. This sofa, Che, was the first thing my grandmother owned in this country—she bought and paid for it with what she made working in the factory. It's not secondhand either.

CHE. No, I can tell—I can see it through the plastic—it's first-rate material.

TEDDY. That spot yer sitting in—was her favorite place on the sofa.

CHE. *(springs to his feet)* Oh, hey, man, I'm sorry.

TEDDY. No, no, siddown, Che.

CHE. You sure? *(looks over at CUBA)* I can sit on the other end. Stand, no problem. I don't wanna desecrate a spot that's sacred. You know, to me all grandmothers are sacred.

TEDDY. You're not sitting on my grandmother, Che.

CHE. I dunno. *(He sits down again.)* It feels kinda lumpy. *(looks at CUBA)* Only joshing, Cuba.

TEDDY. My grandmother used to sit there and read her "novellas" for hours, without budging an inch. Right, Pop? She had stacks of novellas. Remember, Pop?

CHE. I love novellas. They're as bad as the American soap operas. I get off reading them nasty things. You got any around?

TEDDY. No, ...I had to throw 'em out.

CHE. Throw 'em out, why?

CUBA. I told 'im to throw 'em out. They collect cockroaches. *(awkward silence)*

CHE. Cuba, you wanna arm wrestle for five dollars?

CUBA. I'll beat you—

CHE. *(cuts CUBA off immediately)* Put yer money where yer mouth is.

CUBA. I'll beat you over the head with a stick.

CHE. ...Why?

CUBA. What?!

CHE. Why would you wanna beat me over the head with a stick? *(No response from CUBA.)* You wanna arm wrestle? I need five dollars.

TEDDY. I'll lend you the five.

JACKIE. Where's the guy?

CHE. What guy? I'm the guy.

CUBA. *(upset)* The guy you were supposed to bring here—the dealer.

JACKIE. Where is he? *(CHE rises, starts toward the door.)*

TEDDY. You're going?

CHE. I'll be back.

CUBA. *(supset)* Where?

CHE. I told 'im to meet me on the stoop.

TEDDY. Why didn't you initially bring him up with you?

CHE. I wanted to see if it was cool.

JACKIE. It's cool.

CHE. I dunno, Cuba looks like he's mad at somebody.

CUBA. Call 'im from the window. Right here. *(points to the kitchen window)*

TEDDY. It's apartment—

CHE. I know.

JACKIE. Twenty-six.

TEDDY. Twenty-seven.

JACKIE. Twenty-six, twenty-seven, twenty-eight.

CHE. *(Sticks his head out the kitchen window, whistles.)* Come up. Apartment twenty-seven, on the fifth floor. Hurry up. *(to TEDDY)* I'm going up for a movie, yeah, I need to work on something.

TEDDY. How 'bout your writing? You don't wanna write any more plays?

CHE. Naw, man, I wanna be a movie star.

TEDDY. Yer gonna give up writing?

CHE. Yeah, I awready got a Tony Award. What I want is an Oscar. *(Looks at CUBA and at JACKIE, smiles broadly.)*

TEDDY. When are you going up for this movie?

CHE. Tomorrow. You should come with me. You might be right for a part.

CUBA. *(suspicious)* What part is he good for?

CHE. He might be right for a junkie, a mugger.

CUBA. *(stunned)* A junkie? *(to TEDDY)* You wanna be a junkie?

CHE. What's wrong, Cuba? In life, yer a coke dealer, and I'm a junkie.

CUBA. I don't want him playing a junkie.

TEDDY. How 'about if I play a drug dealer, is that better?

CUBA. *(Gives TEDDY a hard look, then to CHE.)* What's taking this guy so long?

CHE. He's got a abscess in his leg. *(slowly for effect)* From shooting coke and dope. *(CUBA and CHE glare at one another. Long pause. With all sincereity, trying to enlighten*

CUBA.) Cuba, you as a dealer, and me as a junkie, we can't live a deeper kinda truth?

CUBA. *(puzzled)* What truth?

CHE. I understand you, Cuba, I understand why you don't want yer son to play the part of a junkie on TV. I understand where you coming from.

CUBA. I'm right.

CHE. We only exist tragically on *Baretta* and *Kojak* reruns. You, Cuba—yer a father, you gotta son, you know, yer doing what you can to raise him—to a lot of people yer nothing but a drug dealer. A nasty cliche. I'm a junkie who steals. I'm a junkie who steals, like a lot of junkies do. But I'm also a junkie who steals with a Tony Award. I'm a junkie who steals, I gotta Tony Award, and I got compassion in my heart for you. *(to JACKIE)* For you. *(to TEDDY)* And for you. I'm a junkie, I steal, I gotta Tony Award—compassion—and I'm Hispanic...that ain't a chiche. The attitude for a junkie like me who is Spanish, is: "Turn him upside down and he got hemorrhoids." It only affects him, and his own kind, and Kojak. I'm a junkie who steals but I got compassion in my heart for the dealer who sells me my dope. *(looks at CUBA intently)* You and I deserve our space. Our time on the air.

CUBA. I feel sorry for you.

CHE. Someone should. But not just for me. For the dealer and the junkie. For both uf us. There's no denying our horns and our tails. Someone should feel sorry for us.

(CUBA stares uncertainly at CHE. Long pause. Sharp banging on the door. CUBA and CHE are oblivious to the knocking. JACKIE

opens the door. The DEALER hesitates in the doorway. He wears a worn cowboy leather vest, dirty jeans, black shoes. He has a large cowboy-style leather hat on his head and carries a cane. CUBA suddenly explodes. He grabs CHE by his lapels.)

CUBA. *(shaking CHE violently)* Are you trying to shame me? *(As CUBA repeats this line over and over, CHE remains distant, calm, allowing CUBA to manhandle him. The DEALER has lifted his cane to strike CUBA.)*

JACKIE. *(To the DEALER, stepping in and grabbing his cane.)* Relax, relax. *(JACKIE and the DEALER both hold on to the cane.)*

TEDDY. Stoppit, Pop, please, stoppit.

CHE. Let 'im. *(CUBA stops shaking CHE but doesn't release him.)*

JACKIE. *(Let's go of DEALER'S cane. Closes the door.)* Cuba, let the gentleman go.

CUBA. *(To CHE, his voice trembling with suppressed fury.)* Are you trying to shame me?

DEALER. *(concerned)* Che? *(The DEALER lifts his cane menacingly. CHE waves it down. DEALER lowers the cane.)*

JACKIE. Cuba, let the gentleman go. We got business here.

CHE. ...You got the gun.

DEALER. *(stunned)* He gotta gun?

TEDDY. He's not gonna use it. *(pause)* Pop?

JACKIE. Cuba, this ain't you. This ain't like you, buddy. *(Long pause. CUBA releases CHE.)* Now, that's more like you. Let's forget what just happened. The sooner we do the better it is for everybody.

DEALER. Let's be sure and lemme see him put his gun

away, far away from me.

JACKIE. Yeah, okay, good idea. I'll feel better too. We'll all feel much better. What do you say, Cuba?

CUBA. *(to DEALER)* Get out. *(slowly for effect)* Get out.

JACKIE. Cuba, that's not what yer supposed to say.

CUBA. Get out. Get out, man. Go. Get the fuck outta here.

DEALER. This man is crazy.

JACKIE. Dramatic-dramatic, he's dramatic!

TEDDY. Che, yeah, you should go. Yes, please.

CUBA. *(to DEALER)* You want something?

DEALER. I came for the pot.

CUBA. There ain't no pot *(He puches DEALER toward the door.)*

JACKIE. *(excited)* I got two pounds.

CHE. *(calmly)* Let's go.

JACKIE. Whacha doin' Cuba?

CUBA. *(to TEDDY)* You wanna go with your friend?

JACKIE. Wait a second, Cuba, these dramatics gotta stop.

CUBA. *(to TEDY)* Go 'head, go with him.

TEDDY. *(hurt)* Why are you saying this to me, Pop? *(CHE and DEALER exit reluctantly.)*

JACKIE. *(throws his hands up)* Whatta we gonna do with the pot?

CUBA. The fucken pot? The fucken pot, Jackie? You haven't heard nothing!!!

JACKIE. Heard what? His friggin' words mean so much to you?!

CUBA. *(points to TEDDY)* It does to him.

JACKIE. Is this gonna be yer normal behavior from

now on? If it is, kiss this coke deal good-bye—I ain't fronting you shit.

CUBA. *(His face is hard, He stares at TEDDY for a second with bitter hostility.)* Get outta my sight. Yer starting to look like this guy, Che. Go to yer room.

TEDDY. No, Pop, I wanna be here with you.

CUBA. Get outta my sight.

JACKIE. Go 'head, kid, go.

TEDDY. I wanna talk to you, Pop. Che didn't say nothin' bad.

JACKIE. I didn't hear him say anythin' to put ya down, Cuba.

CUBA. *(He's confused, losing his temper. Lifting his fist, He turns on JACKIE in a rage.)* No, man, no! *(He quickly turns away from JACKIE and punches the wall instead.)* No! *(He storms out of the apartment.)*

TEDDY. Pop?

JACKIE. *(closing the apartment door)* Dramatic, dramatic, Mickey Rooney never acted so dramatic.

TEDDY. He's been up all night.

JACKIE. He's awright, he jus' snorted too much. I'm gonna go after him, we gotta finish up this coke deal. Take care of my two pounds, don't let the mice get to it.

TEDDY. Rats.

JACKIE. Whatever. Lock the door.

TEDDY. Hurry up, Jackie, my father ain't feeling well.

JACKIE. Don't worry, I'm taking him in the car, he'll calm down when he makes some money.

(JACKIE exits. TEDDY locks the door. He takes a seat on one of the chairs at the kitchen table. Suddenly spent and miserable, he lays his head on the kitchen table. After some time there is a loud scratching on the door.)

TEDDY. *(cautiously approaches the door)* Who? *(no answer)* Who is it?...Who?

(TEDDY looks through the peephole. Opens the door. CHE enters.)

CHE. I was upstairs...on the roof.

TEDDY. What were you doing up there?

CHE. Thinking, man, I was thinking.

TEDDY. Oh, I thought, maybe you were shooting up, or something.

CHE. I'm sorry about your father. I thought I was saying something nice. I think I said it wrong for him to understand.

TEDDY. I want you both to be friends.

CHE. When he's coming back? I saw him and the other guy get in a car.

TEDDY. I dunno, not for a while. *(long pause as CHE gathers his thoughts)*

CHE. Whatta fucked-up scene. Yer father, man, he shouldn't do that. He shouldn't treat people like that, you know? People got feelings... *(He shakes his head from side to side.)* Here's a lollipop for 'im. *(TEDDY takes the lollipop.)*

TEDDY. You and I are still friends.

CHE. What?

TEDDY. We're still friends, right Che?

CHE. Can I siddown?

TEDDY. Siddown, yeah.

CHE. On the sofa?

TEDDY. On the sofa, yeah.

CHE. I'm gonna sit here, on ya grandmother's spot. Where's your spot?

TEDDY. I don't have a spot.

CHE. How 'bout yer father?

TEDDY. He don't have a spot either.

CHE. Jus' me and yer grandmother.

TEDDY. Yeah.

CHE. I always get along with grandmothers. Yeah, we're still friends. I need a friend, it gets kinda lonely, you know, living all alone in the park, it's awright in the daytime, there's lotsa people around. You ought to come down there with me.

TEDDY. And do what?

CHE. Yer with me.

TEDDY. And do what with you?

CHE. Be with me. We don't gotta get high.

TEDDY. No.

CHE. You should come down jus' to be with me. Not because you wanna get high.

TEDDY. Okay.

CHE. We can laugh—we can spend the time laughing. Laughing at the funny-looking trees. You can laugh at me. *(exaggerated)* Ah-hah-hah-hah. You know?...There's a sky up there. I didn't know that until the other night. I was laying on the bench, I aid what's that? A sky, wow. Forgive me, I didn't know you were there. I got scared— it wasn't doing nothing, for a long time, you know? Ah-hah-hah-hah. It's not funny, you know why?...I saw a suicide... *(long pause as he gathers his thoughts)* This ...star...killed itself, did it right before my eyes. Wow. Ah-hah-hah-hah.It's not funny, it scared me. This little star, admitted to itself, I don't like twinkling, twinkling, doing all the work for this sky. You twinkled me out, I don't even shine bright—I'm a fallen star, and that's when I saw it, you know, shoot itself—shooting star...It scared me. If you were there, you coulda held my hand. Ah-hah-hah-hah. It's not funny. Feel. *(He takes hold of TED-DY'S hand.)* It's sweaty.

TEDDY. Hot flashes.

CHE. Ah-hah-hah-hah. *(long pause)* It's nice, right, like this? We got the breeze, the moon, a tree, no one sees us. But we see them. *(No response from TEDDY who feels uncomfortable.)* Yer not holding my hand, it feels limp, why?

TEDDY. ...'Cause yer holding it.

CHE. Hold my hand. *(He releases TEDDY'S hand and offers his own. TEDDY takes hold of it.)* No.

TEDDY. *(confused)* What?

CHE. Like this. *(He interlocks his fingers with TEDDY'S. Like old lovers.)* How's it feel?

TEDDY. *(shrugs his shoulders)* It feels awright.

CHE. No it doesn't...It feels weird.

TEDDY. Yeah.

CHE. I like it.

(A long silence. TEDDY and CHE sit on the sofa, holding hands

like uncomfortable lovers touching for the first time. The DEALER
flings the apartment door open. TEDDY springs to his feet.)

TEDDY. *(panicky)* What's he doing here? He's got to split.

DEALER. *(entering)* What's taking you so long?

CHE. Nothing.

DEALER. Why is it taking so long?

CHE. I ain't taking that long.

DEALER. I'm standing on the roof waiting for you—my leg is killing me. This fucken abscess, I like to cut off the whole motherfucken leg from my neck down, I hate it so fucken much.

TEDDY. You can't stay long.

DEALER. We know.

TEDDY. No, I mean...you.

DEALER. Yer pops ain't here. Be cool. I saw him take off in a car with that, that...fat guy.

TEDDY. Still.

DEALER. *(to CHE)* The pot is here, right?

TEDDY. Why? *(The DEALER looks around the apartment.)* What's he doing, Che?

CHE. I dunno. What are you doing?

DEALER. You know what I'm doing. What you're doing?!

CHE. I ain't doing nothing.

DEALER. I'm way ahead of you.

TEDDY. What does he mean, Che?

DEALER. Think.

TEDDY. Huh?

DEALER. Think.

CHE. I don't want the pot for myself.

TEDDY. I can't give youse the pot.

DEALER. *(to CHE)* You'd fight for the seeds.

CHE. *(He's lying.)* I don't.

DEALER. You didn't take this long 'cause you wanted the pot for yourself?!

TEDDY. The pot is not mine.

DEALER. *(disbelief)* C'mon.

TEDDY. I'm sorry, but I can't sell the pot.

DEALER. I don't wanna buy it.

CHE. He wants to "Bogart" it from you.

TEDDY. *(nervous)* It's not mine. The pot is not mine. It's my father's.

DEALER. *(hard)* I want the pot.

TEDDY. *(frightened)* Okay, but wait for my father—

DEALER. I'm taking it from you.

TEDDY. My father is coming back, talk to him.

DEALER. I'm talking to you. I'm taking the pot from you. You the one got me down here, you the one I'm taking it from.

TEDDY. I don't have it.

DEALER. *(raising his cane)* Motherfucker, I'll hit ya in the mouth wit this. Don't bullshit me. I saw yer father and the other guy come down and they wasn't carrying a fucken thing.

CHE. Don't say yer gonna hurt him.

DEALER. I ain't playing, Che.

CHE. Don't say yer gonna hurt him.

DEALER. Is the pot a big deal to you?

CHE. He's responsible.

DEALER. Tell your pops I took it from you.

TEDDY. I can't tell him that.

DEALER. How come?

TEDDY. I can't.

DEALER. You're gonna have to.

TEDDY. He'll come after you.

DEALER. Then you best tell him something else.

TEDDY. Why?

DEALER. Tell him something else.

TEDDY. Che?

DEALER. Che, what?!...Che, nothing. Che's with me.

TEDDY. Che!...Che? *(CHE walks over to the window.)* Che? *(CHE sticks his head out the window.)* Che?...Che. *(screams)* CHE! *(CHE draws his head back into the apartment and glares at TEDDY.)*

DEALER. You hear what he's saying to you? Shut up, Che, you saying too much. Don't tell him that. *(to TEDDY)* You hear that?...He loves me. *(Awkward silence as he searches TEDDY'S face for a response. He continues to look at TEDDY as he speaks.)* I love you. *(long pause)* Gimme the pot. *(shouts)* GIMME IT!

CHE. Give it to him. Either way he's gonna get it. Give it to him, or I'm gonna give it to him. *(TEDDY reluctantly fetches the knapsack containing the pot from behind the refrigerator.)*

DEALER. *(to TEDDY, mocking)* I love you. *(TEDDY, with great force, throws the knapsack at CHE'S feet. The DEALER laughs as he picks it up. To CHE, heading for the door.)* I got you, awright? I got yer ounces, jus' come over whenever you want. *(He exits.)*

TEDDY. You picked him over me? *(Stunned. Jealous. Hurt.)* You love him?

CHE. I didn't say that.

TEDDY. *(excited)* I saw it!

CHE. I gave him a good rap about your father. You saw what happened, your father fucked up. He was gonna take the pot, blow your father away. I talked him outta that...Life is a game of cards to him.

TEDDY. What about you?

CHE. I saved your father's life.

TEDDY. *(sarcastic)* You love him...You brought him here.

CHE. Yeah, I brought him here in good faith.

TEDDY. Would you hang out and tell my father that when he asks me what happened to the two pounds?

CHE. You tell him what you want, but I saved his life.

TEDDY. What are you getting for robbing me?

CHE. He wants to give me a couple of ounces, that's the way he is.

TEDDY. But you're accepting it—it's your way. Where's the money? *(excited)* Where's my father's money?!

CHE. Would you have given it to me if I woulda asked you?

TEDDY. No.

CHE. Okay.

TEDDY. 'Cause it's not mine to give.

CHE. That's why I'm accepting only what belongs to me. From his point of view.

TEDDY. Nothing belongs to you.

CHE. That's the way it is. Your father knows how it is.

TEDDY. You're an animal.

CHE. I am an animal.

TEDDY. 'Cause you wanna be.

CHE. 'Cause I have to be.

TEDDY. But I'm your friend.

CHE. So you'll understand.

TEDDY. What about me?

CHE. You're still in one piece.

TEDDY. I'm not in one piece.

CHE. Winter is coming, you want me to sleep in the park, to freeze to death?

TEDDY. What are you talking about?

CHE. You would do it to me if you found yerself sleepin' on the streets.

TEDDY. What about this movie?

CHE. I'm only going up for it. I haven't been okayed for the part.

TEDDY. And if you get the part?

CHE. I get the part, yer father and his partner gets their money.

TEDDY. No they won't.

CHE. Why?

TEDDY. 'Cause you have no intention to.

CHE. Why?

TEDDY. You don't wanna pay 'em.

CHE. I'll pay them.

TEDDY. No you won't.

CHE. I'll pay 'em.

TEDDY. You won't.

CHE. I won't.

TEDDY. Why?

CHE. I don't wanna pay them.

TEDDY. Why?

CHE. Fuck 'em. —That's the way it is in drugs. I get a bag of rat poison, I shoot it up, somebody says, fuck 'im. Your father rips off another dealer, he says, fuck 'im. I'm sure he's done it. 'Cause that's the way it is in drugs.

TEDDY. Fuck me too, right?

CHE. That's the way it is, yeah.

TEDDY. I don't want a friend who robs me.

CHE. When it comes to drugs—

TEDDY. Our relationship is not about drugs.

CHE. It's not about you and me.

TEDDY. It is about you and me.

CHE. It's only about you baby—you alone.

TEDDY. Where are you?

CHE. I'm in the gutter. Nine years old. No shoes on my feet. I got 'em in the sewer water. My arm is up like this— *(raises his arm straight about his head)* I'm holding a mango. I'm making believe the bottle cap I'm playing with in the sewer water is really a sailboat. I'm playing— living just to play in the street. Hmmmm. I smell fried pork chops. Hmmm. Fried green bananas. I'm playing, playing in the street. Loving it, until this little girl comes behind me and snatches the mango outta my hand. Now, I don't wanna play in the street no more. *(He lowers his arm.)*

TEDDY. *(after a long pause)* You robbed me. You fucken robbed me, Che. I never knew you were like this,

CHE. ...I always wanted to be a junkie. I always wanted to, you know, tread—on blood.

TEDDY. Ah-hah-hah-hah.

CHE. Yeah, to step in it when I saw it on the

sidewalk...or on the stairs in my building, in my hallway. Man, I'd see it, I couldn't take my eyes offa it. I could hear nothing but the blood throbbing in my ears, and I'd stand, you know, still, lissening to it.

TEDDY. Ah-hah-hah-hah.

CHE. Shut up, man.

TEDDY. I know yer not serious—

CHE. Do you hear?

TEDDY. What, the blood throbbing in your ears?

CHE. I ain't playing with you. I'm tellin' you what I use to say ... What beast died today?

TEDDY. Yeah.

CHE. What beast died today?

TEDDY. And...it was the blood of the beast, and not the blood of a human being?

CHE. You know how I could tell? When I'd see the blood, like say, I'd see it on the stairs in my building, I'd touch it, yeah. I'd stick my finger in it—look at it—and I could tell it was a beast who just died, by rubbing my fingers, like this...The blood would be weak, it would disappear like water. And I knew, a junkie died somewhere. A junkie's blood ain't thick, it ain't healthy, like a red-blooded American.

TEDDY. And that's what you wanted to be, a sick junkie?

CHE. The Beast. Alone...with my own pitch-black sky, my own black reflection, my own withered flowers growing outta the darkness. I don't gotta share it with nobody — nobody wants it. The Beast.

TEDDY. What is this? Is this outta one of your plays?

CHE. *(angry)* This is me, man, this is me!

TEDDY. I don't like it.

CHE. Yer weak. I don't need bread and water, a roof on my head. I can live, man, through winter nights. I don't need to know where the fuck I'm going, why the fuck I'm going? Nobody fucks me, 'cause I'm awready dead to them. Yeah, I like that. Being dead. I ain't there, I ain't here.

TEDDY. A junkie.

CHE. The Beast!

TEDDY. Yeah.

CHE. Yeah.

TEDDY. I'm scared. *(CHE smiles broadly.)* I'm scared of you.

CHE. Ah-hah-hah-hah.

TEDDY. I'm scared of my father. *(CHE strikes his Pachuco pose, swinging his keychain in a circle.)* I'm scared of myself.

CHE. Ah-hah-hah-hah.

TEDDY. I'm scared of people, period.

CHE. I was only teasing you, man.

TEDDY. I am.

CHE. It was all a joke.

TEDDY. But I am, Che.

CHE. Yeah.

TEDDY. I don't want to be.

CHE. Yeah.

TEDDY. I won't be.

CHE. You should be. We were all pushed outta the womb. Nobody crawled out on his own. People are fucken scary.

TEDDY. I tried hitting myself yesterday. I can't do it to myself.

CHE. You wanna be a junkie learn how to hit yerself, become a pincushion.

TEDDY. It hurts, I don't like pain. When you do it for me I never feel the spike going in.

CHE. You want me to show you how to do it, you don't feel the spike going in?

TEDDY. No, I don't wanna learn. Just do it for me. I got three fucking bags. *(He inserts his hand into his pocket, withdraws it. He shows CHE he is holding three bags of heroin.)*

CHE. Whachu gonna do with that?

TEDDY. I wanna do it.

CHE. Why don't you let me do it?

TEDDY. Some, yeah. You fix the shot and hit me, I'll give you some.

CHE. No, I do it all for myself.

TEDDY. No.

CHE. You can't do it.

TEDDY. I know, but you can do it for me.

CHE. I'm not gonna hit you.

TEDDY. You can do most of it. I jus' wanna little.

CHE. I'll hook it up for you—if you do all three bags.

TEDDY. No, I'll OD.

CHE. *(starts for the door)* I'm going.

TEDDY. Okay, I'll do all three bags. Lemme get my set of works. *(CHE doesn't move. He watches TEDDY run into his room, lift his mattress and return with the brown paper bag.*

*TEDDY drops the contents of the bag onto the coffee table. He goes
quickly to the kitchen and returns with a cup of water. He sits on the
sofa. He opens one bag of heroin and proceeds to tap out the contents into the bottle cap. He goes to open another bag.)*

CHE. Jus' do one bag. Hold on to the other two.

TEDDY. *(puts the two bags of heroin in his pocket)* This is
where I need your help, I dunno how much water to put
in. *(He takes the hypodermic and withdraws from the cup.)*

CHE. You need brown water.

TEDDY. *(shows CHE the hypodermic)* This much water?

CHE. Brown, like the sewer water in me.

TEDDY. This okay?

CHE. A little more...

TEDDY. *(Withdraws a little more water from the cup, shows
CHE the hypodermic again.)* Awright?

CHE. *(nods yes)* Show the children, I would show the
children. Cook it up.

TEDDY. *(Squirts the solution into the bottle cap. He lights a
match and proceeds to heat the bottle cap.)* Tell me when?

CHE. When. That's enough.

TEDDY. *(Blows out the match. Withdraws the solution, screws
the needle onto the syringe.)* Here, hit me. *(CHE takes the
hypodermic from TEDDY. TEDDY rolls up his sleeve. CHE makes
a fist and it appears he is going to insert the needle into one of the
veins on his own hand.)*

CHE. How do you get in touch with somebody's
wound?

TEDDY. What are you doing, Che?

CHE. How, huh, without contaminating yerself?

TEDDY. That's for me.

CHE. *(stares down at his fist, searching for a vein)* How do you get in touch with somebody's wound? *(As TEDDY reaches for the hypodermic, he dramatically pulls back.)* Don't touch the wound.

TEDDY. Stoppit, Che. C'mon.

CHE. How do you get in touch with somebody's wound? Don't touch the wound. But Lazarus had dogs to lick his wounds...Commere. Hold yer arm, lemme lick yer wounds. *(TEDDY holds his bicep, tightly.)* Pump yer hand...You'll be like me.

TEDDY. I don't like disliking myself.

CHE. Do something about it.

TEDDY. I am. Why don't you do something about it?!

CHE. I awready have. I'm a junkie. The junkie Christ. *(He inserts the needle into TEDDY'S arm. TEDDY moans.)* Sometimes little lambs gotta be sacrificed, so God can be revealed.

TEDDY. You robbed me, Che. *(CHE pulls out the needle. He stares down at TEDDY with mingled worry and irritated disapproval. TEDDY leans back, nods out. CHE takes the brown paper bag from the table and proceeds to put in it the hypodermic, bottle cap, matches and the torn cellophane paper which contained the heroin. He moves through TEDDY'S room, heading for the bathroom. He returns, sits on the sofa beside TEDDY. He inserts his hand underneath TEDDY'S shirt, rubs TEDDY'S chest.)*

CHE. It feels good...

TEDDY. Mmmmm. *(Silence as CHE continues to rub TED-*

DY'S chest.)

CHE. I robbed you?

TEDDY. Mmmmm.

CHE. I robbed what? I'm too fucken worthy to rob. Now I lay me down to sleep. I pray the Lord, something, something. God bless, Mommie, God bless, Daddy. If I should die before I wake, — I'm goin' in ya pocket. *(Stops rubbing TEDDY'S chest and inserts his hand into TEDDY'S side pocket.)* I'm in ya pocket. That's my hand. My fingers.

TEDDY. Mmmmm.

CHE. I'm taking the two bags of dope...I'm taking my hand out. In the name of the father, and of the son, and of the Holy Spirit, Amen. ... Tell yer father I took his pot. *(CHE stands.)* He knows how it is. He'll understand.

TEDDY. No, I understand. *(CHE takes TEDDY'S hand and smothers it with kisses. He turns and quickly heads for the door.)* I don't wanna see you again, Che.

CHE. No, you shouldn't. *(He opens the door.)* Bye, bye, Teddy Bear.

(CHE exits. Lights dim except for a soft spotlight on TEDDY'S face. His eyes are closed. Music to suggest the passage of time. After several moments, lights come up again.)

JACKIE. *(offstage)* I gotta drop my tank.

CUBA. *(offstage)* You gotta drop what?!

JACKIE. *(off)* I gotta take a leak, Cuba. I'm pissing in my pants—dribble, dribble, dribble.

CUBA. *(off)* What?

JACKIE. *(off)* It's dribbling down my leg.

(JACKIE enters.)

JACKIE. Confucius say: "Man who sits to pee never wets floor."

(CUBA enters and locks the door. JACKIE gives a quick glance behind the fridge. On his way to the bathroom, he points at TEDDY.)

JACKIE. What's this? *(to CUBA)* ...I don't see the two pounds, where is it? Maybe he smoked it all.

CUBA. Go peepee. *(JACKIE quickly exits. CUBA scrutinizes TEDDY.)*

JACKIE. *(Offstage; singing loudly.)* Ninety-nine bottles of beer on the wall, ninety-nine bottles of beer. You take one down, pass it around, ninety-eight bottles of beer on the wall. Ninety-seven bottles of beer on the wall, ninety-seven bottles of beer. Ahhh...

CUBA. *(to TEDDY)* Hey Mister Magoo—wake up.

TEDDY. *(His eyes remain closed.)* Hmmm?

CUBA. *(agitated)* Wake up!

TEDDY. *(slowly opens his eyes)* Pop?

CUBA. Throw some water on ya face—you look nasty.

TEDDY. *(closes his eyes again)* Mmmm.

CUBA. *(smacks TEDDY on the knee)* Are you tired? You tired, you go to bed.

TEDDY. *(opens his eyes wide, surprised)* Pop?!

CUBA. You smoked any of that shit? Lemme smell

yer breath?

(JACKIE returns but remains standing in the passageway.)

JACKIE. Cuba? Cuba, commere a second. *(TEDDY rushes into the kitchen to wash his face.)* Commere, I wanna show you something. Yes, commere. *(CUBA walks over to him.)* Lookit this. *(shows CUBA the hypodermic)*
CUBA. What the hell is that?
JACKIE. You know what the hell it is.
CUBA. Whachu doin' with something like that?
JACKIE. Me?!
CUBA. Where'd you get it?
JACKIE. It was in the sink, in the bathroom.
CUBA. My sink?
JACKIE. That's right.
CUBA. In my bathroom.
JACKIE. In your bathroom—sport fan. In your sink.
CUBA. Are you sure about that? But are you sure?
JACKIE. Are you sure that's your bathroom, and your sink?
CUBA. I'm sure.
JACKIE. I'm sure too.
CUBA. It ain't mine.
JACKIE. It ain't mine either.

(Long pause. CUBA takes the hypodermic from JACKIE. He puts on Agua Florida.)

CUBA. *(moving toward the sofa.)* Teddy siddown over here.

JACKIE. *(also moving toward the sofa)* Where's the two pounds, CUBA? *(TEDDY resumes his seat on the sofa.)* Teddy, where'd you put the two pounds?

CUBA. *(upset)* Wait a second, awright Jackie? Just wait a minute.

JACKIE. First you said a second. Now a minute, make up yer mind. Don't get my hopes up—for a second—if you really mean a minute. *(CUBA gives JACKIE a dirty look.)*

CUBA. *(to TEDDY)* What's going on here?

JACKIE. Yeah, where's the two pounds.

CUBA. Jackie, yer hump!!

JACKIE. Awright, awright.

CUBA. *(calm, choosing his words carefully)* Don't be afraid. I'm not gonna hurt you—I'm on your side. *(TEDDY struggles to keep from nodding in front of him.)* I wanna talk. That's all. Talk. You wanna smoke a cigarette?

JACKIE. I'll give 'im a cigarette.

CUBA. I'll light it for you.

JACKIE. We jus' wanna talk.

TEDDY. *(smokes his cigarette)* Talk about the pot?

JACKIE. Where is it?

CUBA. No, about you. *(quickly, to JACKIE)* I'll get your two pounds. Wait. *(TEDDY drops his head back slowly, rests it on the back of the sofa. Inhales and exhales loudly, trying to regain his senses.)* Why ya sweatin'?

JACKIE. It's the two pounds he smoked. *(laughs)*

CUBA. Open yer shirt. *(TEDDY shakes his head no.)* Open yer shirt for me. *(TEDDY slowly unbuttons his shirt. He nods in front of CUBA.)*

JACKIE. Cuba, pal, I don't wanna be here. This is between your son and you. Get me the two pounds, I leave.

CUBA. *(points to TEDDY)* Will you look at this.

JACKIE. I don't wanna look at 'im. No. *(A long silence as CUBA glares at his son. He shoves him back violently. As CUBA explodes, JACKIE attempts to restrain him.)*

CUBA. Hey, you—you don't nod on me! Who you think I am? I'm your father! *(He paces. Stops, shows TEDDY the hypodermic.)* Is this what you do? This... *(flings the hypodermic at TEDDY'S chest)* Why, huh? Why you do this—for what? What problems you got? Tell me? *(TEDDY lets his head drop back against the top of the sofa. Long pause.)*

TEDDY. *(sings)* Boop-boop-a-doop.

CUBA. A healthy kid. What?

TEDDY. *(sings)* I want to be looooved by you.

CUBA. Wha'?

TEDDY. *(sings)* By you—and nobody else but you.

CUBA. This ain't you.

TEDDY. *(sings)* Boop-boop-a-doop.

CUBA. Wake up! I'll throw ya out the fucken window. I ain't gonna see you like this.

TEDDY. *(sings)* I wanna be kissed by you, by you, and nobody else but you.

CUBA. Who the heck is this? This ain't you.

TEDDY. *(sings)* Boop-boop-a-doop.

CUBA. *(grabs TEDDY by his shirtfront)* This is Che. That's who this is. Che! You make me sick. *(spits in TEDDY'S face)*

JACKIE. Cuba??

CUBA. You're garbage. *(He's still holding TEDDY by his shirt, jerks him onto the floor.)* Throw this garbage out. *(JACKIE moves in to help TEDDY.)* Leave 'im. Leave 'im, Jackie. Let 'im get Che to help 'im. He wants to be like 'im. *(JACKIE stands motionless. CUBA crosses to the statue of La Caridad del Cobre. He glares at the statue, inhaling and exhaling heavily.)*

JACKIE. Cuba, lissen, will you. *(CUBA removes his coyales, his necklaces of colorful beads.)* I mean, I know it's not my place to speak out—

CUBA. *(to the statue of the Virgin Mary)* This is evil. I didn't keep my promise—this is what you do?...You're evil.

JACKIE. It's a statue, Cuba, c'mon.

CUBA. *(Striking the statue with his necklaces so they break apart and beads scatter throughout the apartment.)* Evil! Evil! Evil! It's evil! Evil! *(A very awkward silence as CUBA looks about at the scattered beads on the floor.)*

TEDDY. Pop?

JACKIE. Whacha lookin' for, Cuba? *(long pause)*

TEDDY. Pop?...I decided to do this. I made this decision to shoot up.

CUBA. Shut up! I hate that kinda talk.

TEDDY. You know it, Pop. *(CUBA pulls his handgun from his waist.)*

JACKIE. Cuba, c'mon, pal, no dramatics—I'm leaving.

CUBA. *(to TEDDY)* Commere.

JACKIE. I mean it, Cuba—I'll go. *(He edges toward the door.)*

CUBA. Jus' come over here.

JACKIE. I'm at the door, Cuba—please—don't let me open it. I open it—I'm opening it for good.

CUBA. I said, get over here.

JACKIE. That's it—my hand is on the doorknob.

TEDDY. For what, Pop?

CUBA. Just get over here. *(TEDDY hesitantly walks over to his father.)*

JACKIE. I opened the door—the show is over. *(He exits.)*

CUBA. *(hands the gun to TEDDY)* Take it. I want you to take it. Take it. *(TEDDY takes the gun, holding it gingerly.)*

JACKIE. *(Returns, shuts the door behind him)* I forgot my two pounds. I refuse to be a part of this. I'm not here—go on with the dramatics. I'm gonna look for my two pounds in peace. *(getting angry)* 'Cause I hate dramatics. Everybody wants to be Mickey Rooney—but me!

CUBA. Point the gun at me.

TEDDY. No, Pop, please.

JACKIE. Dramatics, dramatics, nothing but dramatics.

TEDDY. *(looking for guidance and assistance)* Jackie?

JACKIE. *(ignores TEDDY)* Dramatics.

CUBA. I want you to point the gun at me. Right here. *(points to his temple)*

TEDDY. No, Pop. *(He attempts to place the gun down on the coffee table.)*

CUBA. Don't put it down.

TEDDY. I am.

CUBA. Give it to me.

JACKIE. Gimme it!

CUBA. GIMME IT. *(TEDDY turns to hand the gun to JACKIE but CUBA rushes forward and snatches it away from him, grabbing hold of him at the same time.)*

TEDDY. Pop, please. Please, Pop, don't do this.

CUBA. Who you think you fucken with?!

TEDDY. I don't know. I'm sorry.

CUBA. You fucken with drugs. Life and death. You wanna mess with drugs— *(getting angrier)* mess with me. I sell drugs. *(points the gun to his temple)*

JACKIE. Oh, God, Cuba, I gonna faint here.

CUBA. Pull the trigger. Pull it. Push the trigger back. Let's shoot drugs. *(Intense silence. CUBA and TEDDY glare at one another.)*

TEDDY. Please, Pop, I don't wanna do this.

CUBA. I don't wanna do it either.

TEDDY. Let me go, Pop.

CUBA. I can't.

TEDDY. Take the gun away, Pop, please.

CUBA. ...We can't talk.

TEDDY. We can talk.

CUBA. We can't talk.

JACKIE. We talk too much anyway. But I have a question?

CUBA. This is the only way.

TEDDY. No, it's not.

CUBA. For me it is! Now, something's gotta happen.

JACKIE. Why does this always happen to me?!

TEDDY. Like what, Pop?

CUBA. *(angry)* I don't know. I don't know.

TEDDY. Pop, I can't see you—with that pointed at yer head.

JACKIE. For God sake, Cuba.

TEDDY. It's not helping me—Pop. It's not.

JACKIE. You wanna shoot something, Cuba? Shoot the friggin' statue!

CUBA. Something has to happen here.

JACKIE. Something is happening here for Christ sake.

TEDDY. Nothing is going to happen, Pop.

JACKIE. Yeah, stop these dramatics.

TEDDY. Please, Pop, nothing will happen.

CUBA. Something's gotta happen.

JACKIE. Nothing, Cuba—you're not gonna blow yer brains—

CUBA. Something's gonna happen. Something. Something.

JACKIE. Gimme the gun. Nothing is gonna happen.

CUBA. Something?

(JACKIE walks toward CUBA. CUBA yells in frustration, the gun goes off. CUBA drops to his knees, holding the side of his head. TEDDY, sobbing, embraces his father. CUBA breaks down completely. JACKIE stands frozen. Frightened. Inhaling and exhaling loudly.)

TEDDY. *(After some time, he raises his head, turns to look at JACKIE.)* Jackie? *(JACKIE remains frozen in horror.)* Pop? Pop, you're bleeding. *(TEDDY gets up and goes into the bathroom to get a towel. There is an intense moment as CUBA slowly raises his head and sees the only friend he has standing in horror. Still on his knees, CUBA stops sobbing. He falters as he attempts to speak.)*

JACKIE. Kill yourself, Cuba?

CUBA. I never been ashamed in my life.

JACKIE. Killing yourself?

CUBA. I had no choice.

JACKIE. No other choice but to kill yourself?!
CUBA. To do something.
JACKIE. You pulled the trigger.
CUBA. I feel I wanted to die.
JACKIE. And your kid?
CUBA. I didn't know what to do with 'im.
JACKIE. So you pulled the trigger.
CUBA. I pulled it. Yeah.

(TEDDY enters with the towel and a bottle of iodine, a large bandage and a small tin box of bandaids. JACKIE has begun to trek out of the spot he has been standing in. Slowly, awkwardly, he moves to pick up CUBA'S gun. He returns the gun back to its place, underneath the statue of the blessed Virgin Mary. TEDDY cautiously approaches CUBA. He stands at a safe distance away from his father.)

TEDDY. *(hesitant)* Pop?
CUBA. *(referring to his son shooting drugs)* ...Did I do this? *(TEDDY is uncertain, doesn't respond.)* Huh? *(He slaps the bottle of iodine, the large bandage and the box of bandaids out of TEDDY'S hands. He grabs hold of his son's arms, yanks him forward.)* Is this what I did to you? I did this?!!
JACKIE. How the hell, Cuba, did you do that to 'im?
CUBA. *(to TEDDY)* You got somethin' against me?!
TEDDY. You're bleeding, Pop.
JACKIE. You are, Cuba, take care of that, pal.
CUBA. I wanna bleed.
JACKIE. I don't like seeing you bleed. Stoppit, Cuba.
CUBA. *(to TEDDY)* I want you to see it.

TEDDY. I wanna wipe it off. Let me.

CUBA. *(Pause as he considers a way to get through to his son. He glares at TEDDY.)* Where did I spit you?

TEDDY. *(ashamed and a little bitter)* ...Right here, on my face. *(CUBA, keeping a vise-like grip on TEDDY, rubs his face against him, smearing his blood across his son's face. JACKIE reacts strongly.)*

CUBA. That's what you did to me.

JACKIE. Fer Christ sake, Cuba.

TEDDY. *(shocked)* My head, Pop?

CUBA. You did that to me.

TEDDY. *(struggles to break free from CUBA'S hold)* My hair, it'll stick!

CUBA. At least I'm fucken lettin' you know what you did to me.

JACKIE. *(angry)* Wipe it off.

TEDDY. *(struggling)* It burns...

CUBA. Don't wipe nothin'. I wanna see what you done to me.

TEDDY. *(struggling)* It smells...

CUBA. Yeah, that's right. It stinks, what you did to me.

JACKIE. Wipe that off. Let him go, Cuba.

TEDDY. I gotta throw up, Pop. I gotta throw up.

JACKIE. My wife says—

CUBA. *(to TEDDY)* What did I do to you?...Huh?! Wha' did I do to you?

JACKIE. *(Steps in between TEDDY and CUBA and forces TEDDY free.)* You put that friggin' blood on him. Yer hysterical, Mickey Rooney! *(Teddy crosses to kitchen sink and washes his face.)* My wife says—

TEDDY. *(to himself)* Dogs—

JACKIE. I gotta right hand couldn't crack an egg-shell—

TEDDY. Dogs lick wounds.

JACKIE. But I gotta fucken right foot, Cuba, drop-kick yer balls from here to South Brooklyn.

CUBA. *(to TEDDY)* You mad at me?

JACKIE. I'm mad at ya. Trying to put a fucken hole in ya head. You gotta big one awready. You know I hate sex, and violence — I gotta little dick — and a right hand can't crack an eggshell.

CUBA. *(Serious. Tight. To TEDDY.)* Who you mad at? *(No responses from TEDDY.)* Yerself?! I'm mad at ya.

(TEDDY runs out of the apartment. CUBA pursues. They both return, TEDDY entering first, says to JACKIE:)

TEDDY. Jackie!

CUBA. *(entering)* What are you thinking about! *(long pause)*

JACKIE. He's ashamed, Cuba, look at 'im, he's got his head down.

CUBA. *(to TEDDY)* Look at me.

JACKIE. Give 'im some money—it always makes me feel better. *(long pause)*

CUBA. I've been an asshole all my life.

TEDDY. No, Pop.

JACKIE. Let 'im.

CUBA. All my fuckin' life. *(long pause)* What do you think of me? You think of me bad?

TEDDY. No, Pop, I don't.

CUBA. You don't think of me good. You wouldn't be doing this stuff, this dope.

TEDDY. Yes, you're right.

CUBA. Yeah, I'm right, okay. But tell me what you don't like about me.

TEDDY. I like you.

CUBA. *(disgusted, to JACKIE)* He ain't gonna tell me shit.

JACKIE. I'll tell you something—pal. *(CUBA is walking into TEDDY'S room. CUBA briskly looks around. Walking toward CUBA.)* Whacha lookin' for, pal, my two pounds? *(to TEDDY, stopping)* Where's the two pounds—where you got 'em?

CUBA. No, this is what I'm lookin' for. *(Walks past JACKIE, holding TEDDY'S writing pad.)*

JACKIE. *(urgent)* Cuba? *(CUBA is looking through the writing pad.)* Wipe yer head, pal.

TEDDY. What are you looking for, Pop?

JACKIE. Give 'im a towel.

TEDDY. ...Here, Pop. *(CUBA ignores TEDDY, he is too involved in the writing pad.)*

JACKIE. Cuba, hey? C'mon, sport fan, wipe yer head—don't be a hard-on. For me, do it for me. You love me, right? You love me like a little hard-on—wipe yer head.

CUBA. *(Takes the towel, gently wipes his head. To TEDDY.)* Read somethin'. *(hands TEDDY the writing pad)*

JACKIE. *(looks at CUBA'S head)* Lemme see... *(to TEDDY)* Where's the iodine? Gimme the iodine.

CUBA. *(to TEDDY)* Read.

TEDDY. What?

CUBA. Anything—read.

TEDDY. No, I don't want to.

CUBA. I want you to. What the hell'smatter with you? You don't wanna tell me what I've done—you don't wanna read—you afraid!

TEDDY. I'm afraid.

CUBA. Of what?! I'm afraid. Read.

TEDDY. You're afraid, Pop?

JACKIE. No dramatics. *(to TEDDY)* Read the friggin' thing—you wrote it.

CUBA. What are you hiding? I don't hide nothing from you. Help me—I'm asking you, you know? You don't wanna ask me. I'm askin' you—I need help. You wanna help me?

TEDDY. Yes.

CUBA. You love me?

TEDDY. Yes.

CUBA. *(immediately)* I don't believe you. Yer bull-shittin'!

JACKIE. I'll read it to you, Cuba—gimme it. Where is it? *(Snatches the pad out of TEDDY'S hand. To TEDDY.)* After I finish this, I want you to get me the two pounds. *(to CUBA)* What do you wanna hear?

CUBA. What's there—anything.

JACKIE. *(to himself)* Ahhh, what's here, huh? *(turns pages, stops, reads)* Words Said at a Time. By: Teddy Cuba.

CUBA. Lemme hear that.

JACKIE. *(reads)* ...Out of control, my curses—like Mount Olympus—thundered up and jolted the Lord Almighty off his throne.

CUBA. No. Gimme something else.

JACKIE. Give you something else? There ain't much here, pal.

CUBA. *(Walks over to JACKIE, looks over his shoulder.)* What's this... *(reading with great difficulty)* "Please, Pop." right?

JACKIE. Yeah.

CUBA. Read that...What's that about? "Please" what? *(Long pause as JACKIE reads it to himself first.)* Read it to me. Lemme hear it? *(JACKIE looks at TEDDY. He's bewildered. Awkward silence. CUBA does not know what's going on.)*

JACKIE. *(to CUBA)* Siddown.

CUBA. *(suspicious)* What do you mean, siddown?

JACKIE. Siddown.

CUBA. I'm gonna need to siddown.

JACKIE. Siddown. *(CUBA sits beside him on the sofa. Long pause. He starts reading.)* Suddenly the door opens. "Get in there." I go in and I see my brother sobbing on the floor. "Get up on the chair." "Please, Pop..." I plead. "Don't hit me." *(long pause)*

CUBA. Go 'head.

TEDDY. I don't want you to.

CUBA. Read it, Jackie.

JACKIE. *(Long pause. He continues reading.)* "SHUT YER MOUTH," and Pop yanks my underwears down to my ankles. "GRAB THE BACK OF THE CHAIR." "Huh, Pop?" "THIS , THIS," and he slams the back of the chair I'm standin' on for emphasis. I did. I felt a cool breeze hit my spine. I felt his angry breath on my buttocks, and that sent a chill through me. "PUT YOUR UNDERWEARS BACK ON." Then he left the room to wash his hands. I quickly pulled my underwears up and I silently sat on the chair — waiting for him to return and say to me: "Everything is awright. I'm sorry. Go back and play." But he didn't—and he made me feel I had offended him. Done something wrong by being in my underwears. Like I know what I'm thinkin' of doin' to Cookie is just as bad. But never worst than to be accused of fucking with your brother.

CUBA. *(shocked, angry, to TEDDY)* I did that to you?

JACKIE. *(continues reading)* I hold Cookie in my arms—

CUBA. I accused you of that? I said those words?

JACKIE. I try to squeeze the living God out of Cookie—so I can do something evil to him.

CUBA. I don't like hearing this. *(to TEDDY)* Stay here.

JACKIE. *(reading)* No. I think of my father.

CUBA. *(to TEDDY)* If I did do it—I don't remember it.

JACKIE. *(reading)* I love my father. I wanna be a man's man, like him. "What?" Cookie says to me. I hold Cookie closer and I think of what could happen to my father in jail...with long hair...the guards pulling at it — shouting, drug dealer! He yells in pain — I love my father. His hair gets longer — down to his ankles. They tie his arms behind his back with it — I love my father — his feet. I love my father. He yells, NO! They kick him, and call him drug dealer. I love my father. They shove his hair down his throat — choke on it, drug dealer. I love him. I love you I say, when they cut his throat. I love you, Pop. I love you, I love you... *(stops reading)* It jus' goes on like that,

Cuba, you know, I love you, I love you—

CUBA. Yer nuts. You want people to read that?

TEDDY. It's jus' a story—

CUBA. Why you write that? For what?

JACKIE. Don't worry him, Cuba, you know whachu do?

CUBA. Whaddayou want me to say after hearin' somethin' like that?

JACKIE. *(with the pad in his hand)* Don't say nothing. I'll tell ya whachu do. *(show CUBA the pad)* You see here, it says: "And Pop yanks my underwears"? You take it and you go all the way down to the end here—where it says "worst than to be—accused of'"—you know, with the brother— *(quickly)* and you cross it all out—all of it. You keep this here: "I love my father. I wanna be a man's man like him." Beautiful. That's friggin' writing. That you keep. And that other stuff about you gettin' hurt in jail— that can go too.

TEDDY. It's just a story—it's not real.

CUBA. I dunno...I dunno...Why didn't you write a story like, you know, where I jumped in the water somewhere and saved yer life—or something like, I ran into a building that was on fire and I pulled you out? Ha? Or when I use to take you to the Yankees games. The Knicks. I use to take you to the Garden to see the Knicks play. The circus. Anythin' you wanted I tried to get for you. You wanted a horse—I couldn't get you a horse—but what did I get you?

JACKIE. A goldfish?

TEDDY. You put me in a horseback riding academy.

CUBA. How much that cost me?

TEDDY. Twenty-five dollars an hour.

JACKIE. You coulda saddled me for twenty. Lookit that?

CUBA. How much shit did I have to sell to pay them twenty-five bucks an hour? You think things you shouldn't think about.

TEDDY. I know, Pop, I think I'm wrong.

CUBA. Yer hurtin' yerself—yer hurtin' me. Yer imagining things that don't do you any good—don't do me any good. I know you gotta problem—I might be the problem—but how the fuck I'm gonna know if you don't tell me? I gotta find out—finding a needle in my sink when I shave and brush my teeth. Hearing whachu wrote it makes you sound like a freak! What's yer problem, tell me?

TEDDY. I'm the prblem. Me!

CUBA. Whachu mean, me?

TEDDY. Me. Look at me.

CUBA. You don't like yerself? You don't like the way you look. You look like yer mother.

TEDDY. I look white.

CUBA. You look American—yer in America—what do you wanna look like? Yer better off.

JACKIE. I wish my problem was lookin' white. I gotta little dick. That's whachu said, Cuba, ya hard-on.

CUBA. I treated you better than anybody. I didn't teach ya Spanish on purpose. I did that, this way you be something better. You know, better than me. Get a better chance.

TEDDY. I'm...better?

CUBA. *Yeah!*

TEDDY. I gotta better chance? I'm the only kid on the Lower East Side that don't speak Spanish.

CUBA. You think I hurt you doin' that?

TEDDY. I don't like Spanish food.

CUBA. What's wrong with a cheeseburger?

JACKIE. Gimme a pretzel anytime.

TEDDY. Spanish music.

CUBA. You gonna be a dancer?

TEDDY. Spanish people.

CUBA. What?

TEDDY. Spanish people.

CUBA. You don't like Spanish people?

TEDDY. I do—but it's...just...Most of the Spanish people I know that...you know, come here, are—you know—

CUBA. What—say it.

TEDDY. Like you.

CUBA. Like me. *(to JACKIE)* Like me. You hear that? Low-life, he means. *(to TEDDY)* I never stuck a needle in my arm. *That's* low-life. My mother, yer grandmother, she was Spanish.

TEDDY. Yeah, *yes!*

CUBA. Was she like ,me?

TEDDY. No.

CUBA. So you dunno whachu talkin' about. And lemme tell ya, I never had a low-life thing like you had with this kid, whaddayou call 'im.

JACKIE. "Cookie."

CUBA. Cookie. Whadda fucken name!

TEDDY. I'm not ashamed of that.

CUBA. Never.

TEDDY. It's all part of growing up. But it was a story, Pop.

CUBA. It's not true? *(to JACKIE)* That ever happen to you growing up?

JACKIE. I'm Jewish! My worst sexual experience when the rabbi circumcised me—a guinea barber—took much off the top. I gotta postage stamp for a dick.

CUBA. *(to TEDDY)* Are you a junkie?

TEDDY. No, Pop.

CUBA. You ain't a junkie.

TEDDY. No, I'm not.

CUBA. What's that word you like to use? Addict! He hasn't made you an addict?

TEDDY. *(rolling up his sleeve)* Look.

CUBA. No, I don't wanna look. What are you then?

TEDDY. What do you mean?

CUBA. *(slowly for effect)* What are you?

TEDDY. *(slowly for effect)* I don't know what you mean.

CUBA. *(excited)* You don't know whachu are? What are you, tell me?

TEDDY. I'm me!

CUBA. What's yer problem?

TEDDY. I wanna write.

CUBA. What's that gotta do with taking drugs?!

TEDDY. I wanted to be like Che.

CUBA. That don't make any *sense!* *(pause)* I oughta kill that motherfucker for this shit.

TEDDY. It's not Che, Pop.

CUBA. It's me, huh? It's me?

TEDDY. It's my life with you.

CUBA. What does that mean?

TEDDY. It's my life with you.

CUBA. Yeah.

TEDDY. Living with you.

CUBA. Living with me what? I feed you. I all the time ask you how you are—anything hurts you. I always ask you!

TEDDY. It's you being who you are.

CUBA. A drug dealer. You don't like a father who deals drugs?

TEDDY. It's only my life with you.

CUBA. You ashamed of me?

TEDDY. No, Pop.

CUBA. You ashamed? You think I'm an asshole sellin' drugs? I know what I'm doin'. I ain't doin' it to you— Che's doin' it to you.

TEDDY. I know, forget Che!

CUBA. Whaddaya want? *(slowly for effect)* What is it you want? You want me to stop?...Huh?

TEDDY. I just wanna learn about you.

CUBA. You don't want me to stop. *(excited)* What am I gonna do? You think of that? Did you ever think what am I gonna do?

TEDDY. I wanna learn.

CUBA. For what, to write it down, make me the bad guy?

TEDDY. It's me.

CUBA. I dunno, it's somethin'. I dunno, a long time ago I didn't keep my promise.

TEDDY. Retribution.

CUBA. Am I getting away with too much? But I ain't

getting away with anything here. I don't see what I'm gettin' away with—what do I got? *(long pause)*

JACKIE. I'll tell ya what I got. I gotta problem.

TEDDY. It's not here.

JACKIE. What is?

TEDDY. Your problem.

JACKIE. My two pounds?

CUBA. What happened to it? *(No response from TED-
DY.)* Huh?

TEDDY. I gave it away.

JACKIE. Don't tell me you gave it away?

TEDDY. I gave it away.

JACKIE. He gave it away. *(He is up on his feet and
pacing.)*

CUBA. He didn't give it away—

JACKIE. No money?

TEDDY. I gave it away.

CUBA. Who you give it away to?

JACKIE. Nothin'? You gave it away?

TEDDY. Yes.

JACKIE. Yes, he said, yes. Jus' like that—he says: yes, he
gave it away—

CUBA. To who?

JACKIE. Where's the gun—I'm gonna blow both yer
friggin' brains out.

CUBA. He didn't give it away.

JACKIE. Whattaya goin' into business for yerself? Yer
learning—yer learning too fast.

CUBA. Who's got the two pounds?

JACKIE. Why the frig did you do that?!

TEDDY. Anger.

JACKIE. Yer hysterical.

CUBA. What kinda anger?

JACKIE. You're both hysterical.

TEDDY. Anger.

CUBA. Hateful anger. That kinda anger?

JACKIE. I'm hysterical.

CUBA. You're still angry?

JACKIE. *(Excited)* I want my two pounds.

TEDDY. I'm frightened—

JACKIE. *(to himself)* What am I gonna tell this guy? I can't tell 'im nothing. I gotta pay 'im. This is hysterical.

CUBA. *(to TEDDY)* What are you frightened of?

JACKIE. This hurts me. My asshole bleeds over this. That's how much this hurts. Now if you took it—

CUBA. What are you frightened of?

TEDDY. No, Jackie, I didn't take it.

JACKIE. But if you did — an' you sold it, made some money — I can live with that. But give it away? My asshole bleeds.

CUBA. *(to JACKIE, upset)* He didn't give it away. *(to TEDDY)* What are you frightened of?

TEDDY. I'm frightened of people—of what you did.

JACKIE. Where is it then? Who took it?

TEDDY. Shootin' a gun off at your head, Pop.

JACKIE. This is hysterical—

TEDDY. The dealer took it.

JACKIE. I'm gettin' hysterical.

TEDDY. And Che.

JACKIE. *(shouts)* I'm hysterical!

CUBA. Why did you say you gave it away?

TEDDY. I didn't want no one hurt!

Jackie. Hysterical.

Teddy. I'm sorry, Jackie.

Jackie. *(upset)* No! No, I don't like people to say to me I'm sorry. I'm sorry, Jackie, I'm sorry. Take a shit an' fall on it. You show me you're sorry, pal. Send me a Christmas card, every Christmas — until I die — something nice like that. And put some cash in it.

Cuba. Yer hysterical.

Jackie. *(to CUBA)* Let's go, we got business.

Cuba. With who.

Jackie. With this guy, Che—an' the other whachamacallit?

Cuba. What kinda business?

Jackie. Breakin'-head business.

Cuba. I awready broke my head.

Jackie. Who told you to shoot yerself?

Teddy. Pop?

Jackie. What about this guy, Che?

Cuba. What about him? Fuck'im.

Jackie. Fuck him — fuck me. I'm out two pounds that come outta my ass.

Cuba. I almost took my life. Don't tell me your problems.

Jackie. Who told you to shoot yerself?

Teddy. Pop...the gun...the gun...

Cuba. *(to TEDDY) I did it, okay?...I'd do it again. I'd do it a thousand fucken times if I have to. Don't say nothin'.*

Jackie. *(long pause)* You're both friggin' hysterical. I feel like taking a shit and falling on it. Why me, Lord, why me?

CUBA. *(to TEDDY)* Lissen...I see what yer sayin' being frightened ... I did that thing to you — pull yer underwears down — People call you gringo — they don't like you.This guy, Che, yer friend, takes the pot. Drugs, guns, people--life—yeah, it's fucken frightening. Junkies—people like me—we're frightening. Me in jail—I dunno what I'm saying—but... *(Long pause as he gathers his thoughts.)* I never wanted to live on the streets—eat garbage an' shit, beg for money—that scared the shit outta me. *(Long pause as he thinks, tries to get his thought across.)* I don't hide nothin' from you, right? I never did. I sold my shit right here out in the open—in front of you—I never locked, you in yer room or nothin'...Why, tell me why I did that—'cause I'm bad, I don't give a fuck about you? *(long pause)* I am a fuck-up.
TEDDY. No, Pop.
CUBA. No, I am a fuckin' fuck-up.
JACKIE. Lissen to 'im.
CUBA. D'you know what I'm sayin'?
JACKIE. What's he sayin'?
CUBA. It's simple.
TEDDY. Yes.
JACKIE. He's a fuck-up.
CUBA. That's not what I'm sayin'. I'm sayin'—I don't want you makin' my mistakes. I did everythin' in front of you so you could see. See me shit in my pants when the door knocks—cops! Arguing over drugs, money. It's frightening—you be scared, you wouldn't want any part of this shit. *(long pause)* About writing...you wanna write about me? At least yer writing the truth. But...whachu

write, the things you write about me is... *(With a look of dis-approval, he sturggles to get his thought across.)* Are you gonna kill me in stories?

TEDDY. Am I gonna kill you?

CUBA. Are you gonna do that?

TEDDY. No, Pop.

CUBA. Yer not.

TEDDY. *(sweet)* I don't think so.

CUBA. Try not to. People change. I'm not sayin' I'm gonna change — not right away. I wanna eat ... And tomorrow too. But you gotta tell me things. I can't do nothin' with you writing. It's just you and me.

JACKIE. And the friggin' statue.

CUBA. *(Rises, walks over to the statue of the Virgin, stands in front of her.)* I'm sorry, forgive me.

JACKIE. *(annoyed by all this)* Jesus—

CUBA. *(as he makes the sign of the cross twice)* Forgive me. Forgive me.

JACKIE. Christ. Yer hysterical.

CUBA. Beat it—talk a walk—I mean it.

TEDDY. *(Distracting his father to keep him from fighting.)* Pop?

CUBA. *(to JACKIE)* I'm throwing you out.

TEDDY. Pop?

JACKIE. Huh, Cuba?

TEDDY. Jackie?

CUBA. *(to JACKIE)* Huh, what?

JACKIE. You came to me.

TEDDY. Pop.

CUBA. I came to you, yeah.

JACKIE. To help you out—front you coke.
TEDDY. Pop, please, don't lissen.
CUBA. Yer a greedy bastard.
JACKIE. *(excited)* I'm out two pounds.
CUBA. I got problems here.
JACKIE. Myth.
CUBA. Money is all—
JACKIE. *(cuts CUBA off)* Myth!
CUBA. Money is all you care about.
JACKIE. It's shit.
CUBA. I feel like shit. How 'bout you, huh? How you feel? *(He pokes JACKIE hard in the chest with his finger.)*
JACKIE. *(backing off)* You wanna know somethin'? Yer hump!
TEDDY. Please, stop, c'mon.
JACKIE. *(to CUBA)* A lot of time when you talk you spit.
CUBA. Who?
JACKIE. You—you spit.
CUBA. Myth.
JACKIE. Lissen! And every time you spit—I lick it!

(Loud knocking. CUBA and JACKIE panic.)

JACKIE. Cops.
CUBA. *(to TEDDY)* See who it is.
JACKIE. If it's the cops, tell 'em you wanna see a warrant.
TEDDY. What if they're only investigating the gunshot?
JACKIE. Nobody home but us chickens.

(loud knocking)

TEDDY. Who is it?
REDLIGHTS. *(offstage)* Redlights, Redlights, Redlights.

(TEDDY opens the door. REDLIGHTS enters quickly.)

REDLIGHTS. Redlights, Redlights, Redlights! *(He laughs, looking into the serious faces of CUBA and JACKIE.)* Cubita, I'd like to come in...if I could. *(He eases into the living room.)*
CUBA. I'm not sellin nothin'.
REDLIGHTS. I don't want nothin', Cubita.
CUBA. Whaddaya want?
REDLIGHTS. I'm all coked-up. *(smiles at JACKIE)* Thanks to you. *(back to CUBA)* I jus'...you know, I wanna be around my people, you know, you. When I start coming down.
CUBA. I got problems.
REDLIGHTS. I see that, man, I see. Beads on the floor, everybody with long faces. C'mon, Cubita, lemme cheer you up.
CUBA. I'm gonna throw the beads on the floor out. Out in the garbage — off the Empire State Building.
JACKIE. Flush 'em down the toilet like you do to get rid of evidence.
REDLIGHTS. *(picks a bead up off the floor)* These are from yer coyales. Put 'em in a glass of water.
JACKIE. I'm not gonna say nothin'.

CUBA. I'm hungry—I'm tired.

TEDDY. Want me to make you something?

CUBA. *(to REDLIGHTS)* I broke the beads.

REDLIGHTS. Yeah, I see.

CUBA. You don't see nothin'. I see! What happens if I throw the beads in the garbage?

REDLIGHTS. They're sacred, Cubita, you know? *(He picks up a bead.)* Like—you don't fool around with Mother Nature! *(short silence)*

CUBA. Put 'em in a glass of water.

REDLIGHTS. Yeah, papi, it purifies them. It takes out that anger, or whatever it was that made you break 'em. I don't know what happened here. And I don't wanna know. Lemme tell ya, papi, it happens, yer human, you dig? Flesh and blood. Jesus Christ, when he was dying on the cross — he said, Father, why hast thou forsaken me? Yeah, Cubita, it happens to the best of men.

JACKIE. I'm not gonna say nothin'.

CUBA. A long time ago I made this big promise to her. I said let it be on my head. I didn't say on my mother's head—I didn't say on my kid's head. *(slowly for effect)* On my head.

REDLIGHTS. I hear you, Cubita, I hear what yer saying.

CUBA. I didn' keep my promise—this guy here, is shootin' drugs.

TEDDY. *(to REDLIGHTS)* I'm not a junkie. I'm just...It's got nothing to do...forget it.

REDLIGHTS. *(to CUBA)* What did you want? Excuse me, Papi, for coming outta the side of my face, but what did you want? To get away with it?!

CUBA. I want it on me!

JACKIE. I'm not gonna say nothin'.

REDLIGHTS. It's the same thing—if it's on him, it's on you. If it's on you, it's on him. This is his home.

CUBA. You know what I'm gonna do? I'm gonna turn her around—let her face the wall.

REDLIGHTS. Punish her.

CUBA. I jus' gotta do somethin'...I dunno what to do. *(He turns the statue to face the wall.)*

JACKIE. I'm not gonna say nothin'. *(CUBA lies down on the sofa.)*

TEDDY. What do you wanna eat, Pop?

CUBA. I wanna eat—you know what I feel like eating?

JACKIE. Pussy.

REDLIGHTS. I thought you wasn't gonna say nothing?

JACKIE. I couldn't resist.

TEDDY. You want a peanut butter sandwich, Pop?

JACKIE. Any turkey in the house?

CUBA. Turkey?!

TEDDY. We don't have any turkey.

CUBA. Turkey? Oh, shit. *(He laughs, recalling something funny.)*

JACKIE. You got any pretzels? *(CUBA continues to laugh.)* What's so funny?

CUBA. Whatta dirty life.

JACKIE. The turkey's? *(CUBA laughs.)* Huh?

CUBA. My life. *(He smiles broadly, holding in the laughter.)* My mother on Thanksgiving she use to sing "Happy Birthday" to the turkey. *(sings)* "Happy birthday to you."

(Stops. To no one in particular.) "Happy Birthday," she sang to the turkey. I remember...it started out nice—how you say, you know, like, pure—somethin' like that—you know, when I was a kid—watching my mother sing "Happy Birthday" to the turkey. *(sings)* "Happy birthday to you. Happy birthday to you." *(He abruptly sits up and puts his head in his hands. TEDDY has gone to the kitchen and is making a peanut butter sandwich.)*

JACKIE. Gimme an apple—but slice it in fours. Two with salt, two with peanut butter on it. Hold the pickle, hold the lettuce. A glass of milk, a couple of sheets of Bounty to wipe my mouth—you ain't got Bounty, a couple of sheets of toilet paper—and I think I'll be happy...For now.

REDLIGHTS. Cubita, I'm gonna pick up yer beads.

CUBA. *(Lifts his head, snorts loudly.)* No, don't do that—I'll do that.

REDLIGHTS. I wanna do it.

TEDDY. You wanna glass of water to put 'em in?

REDLIGHTS. *(He's picking up the beads off the floor.)* Yeah, gimme a small glass.

CUBA. Redlights, don't do that, get up.

REDLIGHTS. *(continues)* I wanna do it.

CUBA. Why?

REDLIGHTS. I'm your friend.

JACKIE. Don't expect me to get on my knees—I gotta bad back.

(TEDDY returns holding a small glass of water which he places on the floor in front of REDLIGHTS.)

CUBA. Do me a favor, Jackie.

JACKIE. I ain't gonna bend down to pick up beads—forget it.

CUBA. Turn the statue back around for me. *(RED-LIGHTS begins humming a romantic Hispanic ballad. TEDDY crosses to the sofa with the sandwich. He sits on floor near CUBA. He turns and offers sandwich to CUBA who is breathing deeply, trying to fall asleep.)*

TEDDY. Pop? Pop?

(TEDDY looks at sandwich, takes a bite, leans his head back on CUBA, looks out at audience. REDLIGHTS is still singing softly as the lights slowly fade to black.)

END OF PLAY

WARDROBE

CUBA
V-neck white T-shirt
Patterned boxer shorts
Black long nylon socks
White shirt
Red necktie
Black pin-stripe suit
Burgundy lizard shoes
Gold/ruby ring
Gold ID bracelet
Bath towel
Pink fluffy slippers

Bathrobe for backstage
Black slippers for backstage

JACKIE
T-shirt with padding
Short black nylon socks
Blue Hawaiian shirt
Blue plaid shorts
White slip-on sneakers
Gold wristwatch

Grey suit jacket (II)
Navy velour pants (II)

TEDDY
Blue jeans
Belt
High-top sneakers

Jean jacket
Red sweatshirt

Grey shirt (II)

CHE
Dance belt
Tan socks
Pink shirt
Tan pants
Suspenders
Watch and chain
Tan shoes
Black hat

DEALER
Black T-shirt
Blue sweatshirt
Blue jeans
Assorted socks
Distressed tennis shoes
Trench coat

LOURDES
G-string
Panty hose
Bra
Yellow dress
Beige shoes
Gold bracelets
Gold necklace

Gold earrings
Purple/gold jacket

REDLIGHTS
Brown socks
Black nylon singlet
Tan slacks
Brown 50's shirt
Brown leather jacket
Black slip-on shoes
Gold necklaces
Gold watch

MASTER PROP LIST
*(Includes costume props which are marked " * ")*

SINK UNIT (Practical):
Detergent
Sponge
Drainer
Dmall sandwich plate
Coffee cups
Knives, forks, spoons
Dressing on and under

CUPBOARD UNIT:
6 shot glasses
Knives, forks, spoons
Paper towel
Paper towel holder
Dressing on and under
Brown bag
Hairspray
Q-tips
Woolite

REFRIGERATOR:
Full jar peanut butter
1 Lite Beer in bowl with ice
Bottle of Vitamins ⅔ full
Bottle of vitamins ⅔ full with cocaine in plastic bag
Loaf of white bread
Keys on ring
Iron
Cloth doily
2 lbs. pot in bricks

Large ziplock bag
Knapsack

Ironing board
Broom

Wall phone
Wastebasket
Garbage bag

OVAL TABLE
Tablecloth
2 placemats
3 practical chairs
1 breakaway chair
Ashtray
Wrapped red Tootsie Roll Pop
Clean empty coffee cup
Cup and saucer, with coffee
2 new empty match books
Carlton cigarette pack with 1 Carlton
Full Carlton cigarette pack
2 reefers
Small Swiss Army Knife with scissors
The Post or Daily News

SHRINE TABLE:
La Caridad del Cobre
3 strings "Coyales"
Glass ashtray
Quart Bacardi dark rum

Shot glass
Candle
Pictures on and above, including Hail Mary in Spanish
Other statues and dressing, below

SOFA:
Plastic slipcovers
4 pillows

FLOOR LAMP

RECORD PLAYER:
Doily cloth
Record rack
Albums
Doll Ashtray
Pictures in frames
Table lighter, non working

St. Lazarus statue on shelf

TEDDY BED:
Sheets
Bedspread
Pillow
Pillowcase
Small paper bag
Book matches
Syringe
Small rubber band
Bottle cap

Bobby pin
Small wad of cotton
Foil packet heroin
1 pair shoes

SMALL BUREAU:
Dressing in drawers
Dressing on top
1 top spiral notebook, with Teddy's writing
Loose paper
3 pens
Wastebasket

Cuba trousers on hanger
Bills and change in left front pocket
Wallet in back right pocket

CUBA BED:
Sheets
Pillowcase
Pillow
Blankets

CUBA DRESSER:
Long black nylon socks *
Undershirt *
1 pair boxer shorts with holes
1 pair boxer shorts, no holes *
Shoe horn
Towel
Old Spice cologne

Cuba ID bracelet *
Cuba ring *
Small box of jewelry
Kleenex

CUBA CLOSET:
Black suit on hanger *
Matches in right and left pants pockets
1 red necktie *
White shirt on hanger *
1 pair shoes *

BATHROOM SINK (Practical):
Listerine bottle

2 towels on towel rack

WALL SHELF:
Bottle of Agua Florida
Baby powder
Dressing

BATHROOM CABINET:
Plastic bottle of iodine
Small box Bandaids
Box of large gauze pads
Spare comb and hair bands
Dressing

UR PROP TABLE:
1 sucker

Eddie Palmiere Live At Sing Sing, with album and
    sleeve
"Lourdes" purse, dressed *
2 Bic lighters
2 Kools
Pack of Kools
Gram vial with spoon and coke
Pint bottle of rum, sealed
Cane for dealer
"Diana" repeater
Roll-on deodorant
Biology textbook
3 ring notebook
3 strings of pasta beads, tricked to break (II)
3 foil packs heroin (II)
Teddy's jockey shorts (II)

JACKIE PERSONAL:
Small ball cocaine
Plastic sandwich bag
Small box cornflakes
Straight razor
Folded real bills, 1 and 5 and 10
Pack of Camels
Bic lighter
Handkerchief

TEDDY PERSONAL:
Uni-Ball pen
Big comb

CHE PERSONAL:
Watch and chain *
Pack of Marlboro
Matches

ACT II & ADDITIONAL:
.32 revolver
Blanks
Ear protectors

½ McDonalds burger in box
Empty fries pack
Soda cup with straw
McDonalds bag with lots of straws

1 cc syringe, no needle, glued shut

Teddy's keys or ring

Blood
Small sponge
Cup

Blood
Dauber
Cup

Pack of matches

2nd top spiral notebook, with text pgs. 54 - 58

Water, soap, towels for blood clean up
Kleenex

PERISHABLES (Pulled from master list):

EACH PERFORMANCE:
Small ball MANNITE
Sandwich size plastic bag
1 Lite beer
2 slices white bread
Peanut butter
2 reefers
Marlboros
Kools
Carltons
1 empty match cover
1 sealed pint rum
1 Tootsie Roll Pop
Splash of Old Spice cologne (water)
3 strings pasta beads
Dash Bacardi
2 foil packs heroin
½ burger

INTERMISSION PROP SET-UP:
McDonalds bag with straws, burger container with par-
   tial burger, empty fries packet, soda container with
   straw — in front of U.S. section of couch
Hypodermic on sink
Small cup with blood and sponge behind U.S. section
   of couch

Empty rum from shot glass into bottle
Arrange pillows on couch
Remake bed
Put 2nd Act red pad on bed
Remove Teddy's coat
Strike 1st Act red pad
Strike money — top drawer
Strike "works" and cup
Strike everything on table including 2 place mats and
   table cloth
Strike hanger
Put ashtray and matches on table
Put iron on top of fridge
Put ironing board side of fridge with knapsack wedged
   into it
Empty container with ice, strike it with vitamin bottle
Put back 4 shot glasses
Close curtains
Sweep floor
Set 4 chairs into table
Reset works in bag and put it under mattress
Hand Teddy 3 "dime bags"
Put Teddy's keys in front door

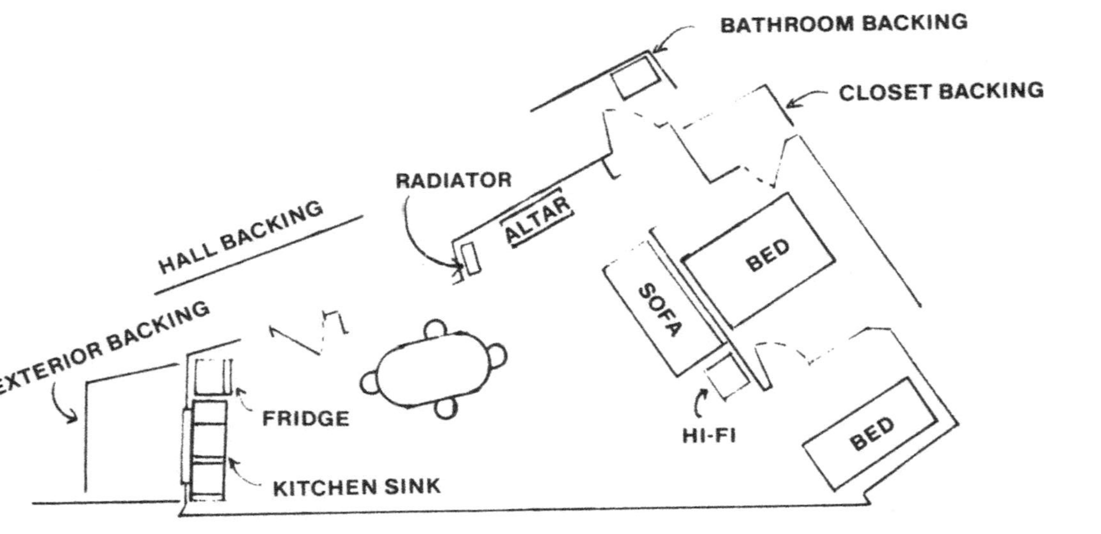

CUBA AND HIS TEDDY BEAR
GROUNDPLAN

About the Author

Reinaldo Povod was born and raised on the Lower East Side of Manhattan. He won the Oppenheimer/Newsday award for *Cuba and His Teddy Bear*, which was his first play. His second play, *La Puta Vida Trilogy*, was given a reading at the Sundance Institute Playwrights Laboratory in the summer of 1985 and was produced by the New York Shakespeare Festival in the 1987-88 season.